The Whistling Thorn: South Asian Canadian Fiction

The Whistling Thorn: South Asian Canadian Fiction

Edited by
Suwanda Sugunasiri

Mosaic Press
Oakville-Buffalo

Canadian Cataloguing in Publication Data

The Whistling Thorn

Includes bibliographical references.
ISBN 0-88962-547-6

I. Short stories, Canadian (English) - South Asian - Canadian authors.* 2. Canadian fiction (English) - 20th century.*
I. Sugunasiri, Suwanda H.J.

PS8329.W55 1994 C813'.0108895 C94-932147-8
PR0197.33.S6W55 1994

Published by MOSAIC PRESS, P.O. Box 1032, Oakville, Ontario, L6J 5E9, Canada. Offices and warehouse at 1252 Speers Road, Units #1&2, Oakville, Ontario, L6L 5N9, Canada and Mosaic Press, 85 River Rock Drive, Suite 202, Buffalo, N.Y., 14207, USA.

Mosaic Press acknowledges the assistance of the Canada Council, the Ontario Arts Council, the Ontario Ministry of Culture, Tourism and Recreation and the Dept. of Communications, Government of Canada, for their support of our publishing programme.

Cover design by Susan Parker
Typeset by Jackie Ernst
Printed and bound in Canada
ISBN 0-88962-547-6

In Canada:
MOSAIC PRESS, 1252 Speers Road, Units #1&2, Oakville, Ontario, L6L 5N9, Canada. P.O. Box 1032, Oakville, Ontario, L6J 5E9

In the United States:
Mosaic Press, 85 River Rock Drive, Suite 202, Buffalo, N.Y., 14207

Dedication

- to the Peaceful and Quiet Revolution of Canada

    through which Canadians have collectively
    worked towards building a promisingly
    multicultural society.

- to MOTHER, Misinona Warnakulasuriya

    who defied death to see a son
    settle into married life.

to FATHER, S H Sauris Silva

    who, by example, inculcated
    a discipline to make the best
    possible contribution to society.

Acknowledgements

I wish to acknowledge with thanks permission to publish or reproduce the following stories:

IQBAL AHMAD, for "The Kumbh Fair," first published in *The Fiddlehead*, 1969, reprinted in *The Opium Eater & Other Stories*, Cormorant Books, 1992;

CYRIL DABYDEEN for a revised version of "Calabogie" which first appeared in *To Monkey Jungle*, Third Eye, 1988;

HUBERT DE SANTANA for "Dublin Divertimento" (unpublished);

LAKSHMI GILL for "Carian Wine" (unpublished);

ARNOLD HARICCHAND ITWARU for "Matins" (unpublished);

SURJEET KALSEY for "Mirage in the Cave" which first appeared in *Canadian Fiction Magazine*, 1976;

MACMILLAN CANADA for Neil Bissoondath's, "The Cage" which first appeared in *Digging Up the Mountains*, Macmillan Canada, 1985;

ROHINTON MISTRY for "Lend Me Your Light" which first appeared in *Toronto South Asian Review*, 1984;

UMA PARAMESWARAN for "The Door I Shut Behind Me" from *The Door I Shut Behind Me*, Writers' Workshop, Calcutta, 1990;

SASENERINE PERSAUD for "When Men Speak That Way" (unpublished);

M G VASSANJI for "A Tin of Cookies" (unpublished);

HILDA WOOLNOUGH for Reshard Gool's, "Operation Cordelia," *TSAR*, 1983.

Contents

Bows & Handshakes

Long in the making, as all anthologies are, this effort would not have seen the light of day without the co-operation of many. The first and foremost, of course, are the writers themselves, who placed their confidence in me in allowing the inclusion of their works. To them I bow with the deepest respect.

But my first bow has to be to Howard Aster of Mosaic Press who invited me to take on the task. It is to Herbert de Santana's creativity that I next bow for the title.

To Tamara, my daughter, I bow for her assistance at the computer at various stages of the manuscript, and to son Shalin, for the quiet understanding of my work.

Swarna I embrace in love and gratitude for her unending patience as I worked through the various stages of this work.

Suwanda Sugunasiri
Toronto
March 10, 1994

Selections Introduced

This anthology represents the works of short ficion written by Canadians of South Asian origins over the last two decades or so. In making these selections, I have sought to introduce the reader to a representative sample of the genre, from the earliest written in Canada in English, Ahmad's "The Kumbh Fair" (1969) to the latest, de Santana's "Dublin Divertimento." Some of them are published here for the first time. While some of the writers, such as Bissoondath, Dabydeen, Mistry and Vassanji, are well-known, my intent was to present the many others as well who have been helping to build the pillar in their quiet ways. Needless to say, there are many others who deserve to be included, but have not been for various reasons, some beyond my control, and I wish to apologize to them. If there are only three women writers here (Gill, Kalsey and Parameswaran), it is not unreflective of the larger reality of the South Asian Canadian scene. It may not be insignificant, however, to note that the characters in nearly half of the stories are female.

As the label, "Canadian of South Asian Origins" indicates, you will, within these pages, find yourselves walking in many lands, beginning with the mainland of India itself, teeming with its various sensibilities. If in Ahmad's "Kumbh Fair" we encounter a woman forced into a decision between prostitution and poverty, Parameswaran, in her "The Doors I Shut Behind Me", introduces us to Indian (Hindu) emigres in Toronto caught in the matrix of two cultures, and unable to decide. Mistry's protagonist in "Lend Me Your Light", from Bombay's Zoroastrian community in Toronto, is more decided. Though not situated in any particular geographic context, Kalsey's surrealist "Mirage in the Cave" presents the plight of an ostensibly Punjabi woman at the hands of a husband whose name ironically is 'Mokshdev', or 'god of liberation'!

It is now a short flight to Sri Lanka where we meet in my story, "Fellow Travellers", three women, ostensibly Buddhist, in their caring and uncaring relationships.

The West Indian urban life is presented in Persaud's "When Men Speak That Way" where a wharf clerk, drawing upon the Hindu tradition of his ancestors, successfully retains his calm working among 'thiefadores', a legacy from colonial times.

Gill's "Carian Wine" and Vassanji's "A Tin of Cookies", both set in Canada, have really very little that is South Asian in them. Gill's is a story of how a family deals with an alcoholic father, while Vassanji's is about an elderly woman trying to shed the image of being "a mean and selfish old woman".

If the South Asian experience in the wider world context provides the backdrop for stories such as the above, those by Gool, de Santana, Bissoondath, Dabydeen and Itwaru have no trace of any such sensibility, indicating just how elastic the 'South Asian' boundaries are. The late Gool's "Operation Cordelia" is a spy-type story set in Britain pivoting around the rich, while in "Dublin Divertimento", de Santana takes us into the working class life of the Irish, sorely ignored by mainstream writers. Bissoondath's "The Cage" is the lifestory of a young Japanese woman who bucks tradition only to wake up to the rude reality of the life of North American women during her short stay in Toronto as she encounters a young woman who gets a 'tit job' done!

In Dabydeen's "Calabogie", named after a place near Ottawa where the story takes place but truly universal, we have one of the most beautiful and symbolic treatments of love. And finally we have in Itwaru's "Matins", a woman, of any and everywhere, desperately, but mockingly seeking to understand God's love in the face of personal disaster.

The characters in these stories, like the whistling thorn tree in the African bush, live their quiet ways in the wilderness of life, whistling paeans of joy and bearing the thorns of pain, roots reaching out to wherever they would find sustenance.

Our authors, too, show that they can sing in the face of any wind, be they Canadian or other, but be sharp as a thorn.

South Asian Canadian literature, finally, can also serve as a thorn in the flesh of the Canadian literati, unless their songs are listened to with the seriousness they deserve.

We then invite you to take this journey, through the pages of *The Whistling Thorn*, to wherever it takes you.

Suwanda Sugunasiri
Toronto, Canada
August, 1992

1

Dublin Divertimento

by
Hubert de Santana

Born in Nairobi to Indo-Portuguese parents, Hubert Ribeiro de Santana was educated in Kenya, England and Ireland. He emigrated to Canada in 1975, and has been a freelance writer specializing in travel and the Arts. Winner of the 1984 Antor Award for Excellence in Travel Writing and a 1985 Gold Award from the Pacific Asia Travel Association, he is a talented artist, and a photographer. A major exhibition of his paintings was held at Gallery Louise Smith in Toronto, and he is the author of Danby: Images of Sport. He lives in Mississauga, Ontario.

My landlady, Mrs. Consolata Carmody, carried her cigarettes in a plastic soap dish, and used a snippet of knicker elastic as a bookmark. She spent the mornings cooking, and the afternoons in bed, sitting on a vast Victorian chamberpot, knitting. In the evenings she sat be the fire in the breakfast room, reading *Butler's Lives of the Saints.*

She was absent-minded. Many a time I had passed the open door of the toilet and caught a glimpse of her sitting in the attitude of Rodin's *Thinker,* unaware of her exposure. She watered her geranium by standing the pot in the toilet bowl. She often forgot it there, and it received a second watering when a boarder "with the drink taken" staggered into the bog for a late-night pee.

Mrs. Carmody was not fastidious. Jellies were left under the hedge to set, and were served decorated with bird droppings. Meat was kept unwrapped on the cellar floor, where mice could inspect it. One day she cut her thumb while cooking, and the soup was thickened with her blood. When I complained about this, her cheerful response was, "Ah sure, it'll do you no harm to get some good Kerry blood inside of you!" I was unconvinced of the benefit of such a transfusion, so Mrs. Carmody scooped up the blood with a spoon and fed it to the budgerigar.

She was not sentimental. When it was discovered that Siobhan, a friend who was on a visit from the country, had died in her bed, Mrs. Carmody looked at Siobhan's uneaten breakfast and said, "Ah, curse her hide! And I'm just after cooking an egg!"

She did not believe in progress. Her only son, Declan, had emigrated to America, where he became a successful bus driver in Boston. Anxious to share his new affluence with his parents, Declan had sent them a refrigerator, an iron, and a toaster. but Mrs. Carmody had no interest in raising her standard of living: "What was good enough for our fathers is good enough for us," she declared. She would not use an electric iron because the current would dry up the blood in her arm and leave it paralysed. And she preferred to make toast by the traditional Carmody method: dealing slices of bread into the fire like a pack of cards. She used the fridge as a storage cupboard, and pawned the iron and toaster.

She was not a gourmet. Her cooking was a catalogue of crimes against the palate. Her Irish stew was a greasy grey sludge containing a few scraps of mutton fat and gristle. Cabbage was boiled into a sour green puree; potatoes crumbled at the touch of a fork. Her pastries and soda bread were as hard and heavy as concrete. The tea she served in cups the size of small buckets tasted like stewed water from the River Dodder.

Her husband, Mr. Padraic Carmody, was in his seventieth year, but his strong body, hardened by a lifetime spent in the fields of Kerry in all seasons, showed no sign of frailty. He had retired to Dublin to see out his days in the boarding house he and his wife owned and ran in Belgrave Road.

Mr. Carmody's fog coloured hair stood on his head in a point. like the head of foam on a pint of Guinness. Nicotine had browned his moustache so severely that it looked burnt. His eyes were a dark grey, as dull and cold as slate. His great beak of a nose gave him the profile of a fierce old bird of prey. Mr. Carmody had an aversion to soap and water, which meant that you had to move to windward whenever he approached.

He was a Roman Catholic with an ignorant, invincible faith tempered with grotesque superstitions. He accepted without question not only all that was taught by priests, but the local folk tales as well. And so he would talk with equal conviction of Christian mythology, and also of the strange green lights he'd seen burning on Macgillycuddy's Reeks; and the little dog that had turned into an elephant on a lonely country road near Cahirciveen; and how he'd seen the Devil move into the Black Church with all his belongings one midnight.

The Black Church was Protestant, a puddle of grey stone with a spire like a dunce's cap. It stood adjacent to the Carmody's house, which distressed them, mainly because the Devil lived in it. If you wanted proof of the black gentleman's presence, said Mr. Carmody, all you had to do was hop around the church on one leg at midnight, reciting the Our Father backwards. When you had been round the church three times without missing a step -- or a word -- you'd find him standing next to you, stinking like a starfish left out in the sun, and wanting to shake your hand. If the ritual did not always work, it was only because the Devil was more partial to Protestants like himself.

The third member of the Carmody triumvirate was Finnegan, a malodorous dog of indeterminate breed, with a wild, curly, matted black coat which gave him the appearance of a prehistoric sheep. The Carmodys optimistically claimed that this canine cocktail was a pure-bred Kerry Blue.

Finnegan was a dog unique in many respects, chief of which was his fondness for consuming his own ordure. This meant that his kennel and compound never had to be cleaned, which the Carmodys considered very fortunate. Finnegan did not need the special care that less robust breeds require. He was kept in his wooden kennel in all weathers, and when his paws froze in the winter, Mrs. Carmody thawed them out by pouring hot tea over them. During these libations Finnegan would howl mournfully, and the Carmodys interpreted this as an expression of gratitude.

He was given a bath once a year by being tossed into the Dodder, before being sheared.

Every Sunday, when the bell of the Black Church tolled, Finnegan howled in a way that congealed the blood of the faint-hearted within a one-mile radius of his kennel. But Mr. Carmody was no Baskerville, and congratulated himself for owning a

Catholic dog which made no secret of its dislike of a Protestant bell.

Finnegan had lost the use of some of his vital masculine functions, and one afternoon I was amazed to see him attempting to couple with a bitch that had wandered into his enclosure from a neighbouring garden. Finnegan had mounted her and, prompted by some long-dormant instinct, thrust himself forward with an energy that made his matted locks leap. But he was no longer equipped for sports best left to the young, and during his ineffectual exertions, the bitch merely sniffed delicately at the inedible contents of his feeding bowl. Then, with callous indifference, she detached herself from him, leapt over the garden wall, and was gone. Finnegan curled up under the apple trees to sleep away his dejection. I called this poignant episode "Finnegan's wake."

* * *

James Corrigan walked into our digs as if he owned the place, put down his two Samsonite suitcases, smiled at the assembly of men gathered in the kitchen for breakfast, and said, "Hi. I'm Jim." The men grunted their greetings. I'd say he's been coddled all his life, and never knew what it was to go hungry. He was wearing an expensive sheepskin overcoat with a thick, creamy fleece. He exuded money, and looked as if he could afford to stay at the Russell or the Gresham.

But none of that for your man James. He'd come to Ireland to mingle with the natives, and he was going to rough it in a Dublin digs while he attended university. Then he'd go back to Toronto and have his rich friends roaring about the Irish and their quaint old ways.

So here was this Canadian with his carefully combed blond hair, healthy complexion, and mild grey eyes, who'd been on a long transatlantic flight from Toronto to Shannon, a tedious train journey from Limerick to Dublin, and a taxi ride -- an unheard-of luxury for a student -- from Kingsbridge Station to Belgrave in Rathmines. And he looked as fresh as if he'd come in from a walk in the Dublin mountains. Only he smelled of after shave lotion instead of heather.

James Corrigan had come to Ireland for an education, and he got one, I can tell you. It began when Mrs. Carmody came forward to greet him. Bandy-legged, her blue eyes sparkling, her white hair whisked up like a conical meringue, she took his hand in hers.

"You're very welcome!" she said warmly, her smile revealing loose false teeth. "Con Carmody's my name." She did not bother to introduce her husband. "Your rent'll be five pounds a week, and that'll get you three meals a day, a bath once a month, and your laundry thrown in as well. You'll not find better digs anywhere in Dublin."

"That's fine. But I'd prefer a bath every day, if you don't mind."

The men at the table snickered. These fastidious North Americans were always good for a laugh.

"God bless us and save us! A bath every day! Sure, you'll be spending half you life in the ould bathroom." Mrs. Carmody was aghast.

" 'Twas the Devil himself invented baths," growled old Mr. Carmody, taking a blackened pipe from his mouth, "and the English that used them to kill us off when they found there was some of us left over from the Famine. Cleanliness is next to godliness, they said: and what would Protestants know about godliness? But there's always Irishmen willing to listen to voices from across the water. They were scrubbing themselves in no time at all, and it was a catastrophe for the country. They died like flies: of TB, pneumonia and exposure. There's nothing like a good layer of dirt on your body to keep the germs away. Wash it off, and you're asking for trouble. I get into the ould tub no more than once a year, and I've never been sick a day in my life."

"Ah sure, the boy must be starving after that long journey of his," broke in Mrs. Carmody, rescuing James from the old man's blather. "Sit down here, like a good soul, and I'll soon have a hearty breakfast inside of you. You'll get no dainty cooking in this house, but only what'll put the flesh on you, though it's not more weight you're wanting, from the looks of you." She looked him over with an expert, approving glance, like a farmer's wife appraising a prize bull at an auction.

James sat down at the table, which had a sheet of zinc over it as a tablecloth. The chairs were crude, with seats of sisal string. The poor sod was going to have to revise whatever romantic notions he had entertained about the Irish. Mrs. Carmody served him her "hearty" breakfast: a tiny soft-boiled egg, a slice of warped and charred toast, and a bucketcup of Dodderwater. James was about to fracture his egg when Mrs Carmody ambushed him with an important question.

"Have you got the Faith?" she asked, sitting down opposite him.

"Pardon me?" He looked confused, and I can't say I blame him.

"Have you got the Faith?' repeated Mrs. Carmody: "Would you be a Catholic, like?"

"I'm a lapsed Catholic," James replied carelessly.

"Lapsed, is it?" Mrs. Carmody said frostily. "Well, you'll just have to unlapse yourself if you want to stay in this house. If you were baptised, you have the mark of Christ on you soul. Once, a Catholic, always a Catholic. And why did you stop going to church at all? You wouldn't be an atheist now, would you? Because if you are, you needn't bother to unpack your luggage -- you can go straight out and find yourself another digs."

James stared at her as if he couldn't believe what he'd heard. But there was no mistaking the angry gleam in Mrs Carmody's eyes; and as for her husband, he seemed to be looking about for a suitable weapon with which to dispatch an atheist.

"Take it easy, Mrs. Carmody," James said, as he put down his spoon. "I'm no atheist. I just never bothered with religion, that's all. I'll be happy to go to church on Sundays, if it means that much to you."

"And it's pleased I am to hear it," Mrs. Carmody said, relieved. "You can start this Sunday: there's the Rathmines Church, and the Rathgar Church, both with Masses every hour on the hour. I've no prejudices, mind: "I'll take a Protestant" -- she pointed at me -- "I'll take a darkie" -- she indicated Rico Delgado, a black West Indian -- "I'll take a drinking man" -- she waved at Tom Neary, and obese alcoholic -- "I'll take a man who'd not quite right in the head" -- her finger jabbed at Fergus McFadden --"but I'll not let an atheist in me house!"

That settled, we proceeded with our interrupted breakfast. James seemed to be in a state of shock, and his eyes were fixed on Mr. Neary. I suppose Tom Neary did take some getting used to. His nose was a purple potato, and his large, flabby cheeks were covered with a network of red veins. His piggy eyes were bleary and bloodshot. His toothless, drooling mouth hung open, and his tongue lay on his chin like a pink apron. A rime of dried saliva made a tidemark at the corners of his mouth. Voluminous trousers shelled his body up to the armpits and, although his fly was open, it didn't matter, because all that could be seen was his chest. Tucked into the trousers was a stained shirt which stank of vomit, and over that was a cardigan with only one button fastened, under considerable tension. His close-cropped white hair glinted like hoar frost on the pink pumpkin of his head.

A thunderous fit of coughing seized Mr. Neary and left him panting sourly over the table. He picked up his soft-boiled egg, stuck a fat finger through the shell, and licked the yellowed digit. His mouth funnelled as he put the egg to his lips and sucked out the contents. He held the eggshell up to the light to make sure it was empty, tossed it aside, and dipped a slice of toast in his tea. Dangling the dripping toast aloft, he let it plop into his mouth where it was churned noisily as he rotated his tongue like the blade of a dough mixer. Then the mess was swallowed with a gulp that made his adam's apple leap.

The rest of us ate in uncompetitive silence.

James Corrigan had polished off his breakfast and was getting up from the table when Sally Noggin bustled in. Mrs. Noggin was a widowed tinker who had given up her nomadic ways in order to look after her bedridden father in a tenement on the north side of the city. She earned her living as a charwoman, and once a week she came south to Belgrave Road and swept through the Carmody house like a whirlwind.

Her grey hair was like steel wool, with a tight crinkle in it. Her small, bright eyes had the darting look of a ferret, and were set in a leathery, dun-coloured face crabbed with innumerable wrinkles. She had a massive bosom, and the muscles of her burled red legs were harnessed in holey stockings.

"Me father's balls is shrunk to nothin'," she announced in a high, reedy cackle, as she stripped herself of a grubby raincoat.

"Shuttup, you walking Brillo ad!" flashed Rico Delgado.

"Hold your balls, you little blackie!" barked Mrs. Noggin, and was about to let fly at Rico with her shoe when Mrs. Carmody calmly intervened.

"Sit down to your tea, girl."

It was more of a command than a request, and Sally complied. But no sooner had Mrs. Carmody tilted the teapot, than Sally was on her feet, gaping incredulously at the pale Dodderwater.

"Christ! We'll need somethin' stronger than that to keep our fannies goin'!" she wailed.

Mrs. Carmody winced, and added six heaped teaspoons of powder-leaved tea to the brew. This black syrup soothed Sally's discerning palate, and after a few refreshing sips she fell back in her chair and gave a gargly laugh of contentment, making a sound like an emptying drain.

"You ever thought of joining de Fire Brigade, woman?" Rico inquired innocently.

Mrs. Noggin's ferret eyes narrowed with suspicion. You had to watch yourself with these foreigners.

"And what would I be doin' that for?"

"Because it a damn shame to waste de ladders in your stockings!" chortled Rico, and fled from the room before Sally could throw something at him.

* * *

Mr. Carmody was an early riser. He emerged from his bedroom with a brimming chamber pot in each hand: his and hers. Slowly and carefully he descended the lino-covered stairs to the bathroom. There were two loud splashes as he emptied the pots into the toilet bowl, followed but the roar of the toilet being flushed. That done, he attended to his oral hygiene by removing his false teeth and giving them a quick rinse under a tap in the washbasin.

"Poo-poo-poooo!" carolled the old man as he came out of the bathroom and tramped heavily down the remaining stairs, past an umbrella stand full of walking sticks, to the kitchen.

That was the signal for me to get out of bed and perform my ablutions.

The only ventilation in the bathroom came from a porthole which blew a draught of cold air down the neck of the person sitting on the toilet. An outdated telephone directory provided toilet paper for the enthroned. The bowl was so close to the bath that if you wanted to shampoo your hair while bathing, all you had to do was lie back in the tub and pull the chain.

There was no hot water in the bathroom taps, except on bath nights. Every morning I took my place in the queue of dishevelled boarders who stood by the stove, holding shaving mugs with scab-like scars where the enamel had chipped off. They looked like mendicants with begging bowls. As each man shuffled up to her, Mrs. Carmody doled out hot water from a battered kettle on the stove.

First in line was Fergus McFadden, a paranoid old duffer who had lost his thumbs in an accident with a threshing machine. For reasons known only to himself, Mr. McFadden was convinced that he was a marked man, with nameless killers closing in on him. He hardly slept at all, and wore out the linoleum in his small room as he paced to and fro all night with a poker at the ready, waiting to confront his murderers.

Occasionally Mr. McFadden's vigilance slipped. One morning he staggered into the kitchen with his trousers down, and wildly informed Mrs. Carmody that an assassin hidden in the bathroom had injected him with deadly germs as he was about to sit on the toilet. He turned his bare bottom to Mrs. Carmody and pointed to the site of the fatal injection.

"If it's going to die on me you are, have the daycency to do it in your own room," Mrs. Carmody said impatiently. "And with your trousers fastened," she added as an afterthought.

Next in line was Rico Delgado, a Trinidadian student who filled the digs with Caribbean warmth. I was saddened (but not surprised) when Rico told me of his long and demoralising search for lodgings in Dublin: he'd been received with suspicion and hostility by xenophobic landladies who'd slammed the door in his face with a muttered, "God help us, it's a blackie!"

When he arrived at Belgrave Road, Rico was pleasantly surprised to find that Mrs. Carmody appeared to be colour-blind. But to make assurance double sure, he shrewdly advised her that he was a Catholic. "Ah go 'way!" she exclaimed. "Where would a darkie like yourself get the Faith?"

"From the good Irish missionaries in Trinidad," Rico answered promptly.

"Come in, so," Mrs. Carmody said courteously.

Rico had later gone to a local pub to celebrate his admittance to the digs. He'd gratefully dropped a sixpence into a coin box on the bar counter. It was a collection for Irish Catholic missions overseas, and it bore the legend: YOUR GIFT WILL HELP SAVE A BLACK BABY FOR JESUS.

I was next in the hot water queue, followed by Jim Corrigan. Once he had settled into the digs, he'd turned out to be a congenial companion. I'd been intimidated by his wealth and self-assurance, but he didn't flaunt his money in the vulgar way that some North American visitors did. Nor was he stingy: he often treated Rico and me to enormous Indian dinners at the Golden Orient restaurant in Leeson Street; and when we went to a pub, he always insisted on paying for our drinks.

He never complained about the primitive living conditions, but when he found the insides of his shoes furred with a green mould, he persuaded the Carmodys to let him use a small paraffin heater in the bedroom. It was as ineffectual as a candle in the brutal Irish winter, but the Carmodys warned that no good would come of sleeping in a room with tropical temperatures.

There were other deprivations which Jim found more difficult to adjust to. He soon learned that Dublin is not one of the fleshpots of Europe, and he was in danger of sexual starvation when one of his friends at University College told him of a glamorous whore named Niamh* Cassidy, who could provide him with a cure for his frustration. By a happy coincidence, Niamh lived across the street from our digs, and whenever she was between customers, Jim went haring over to her flat to make sure that she was not lonely or unemployed. Niamh was always willing to accommodate him, for he paid handsomely. "No rest for the wicked," she would say with a smile, as she let him in every sense of the term.

On Sunday mornings, when Jim was obliged to vacate the digs and make a pretence of going to Mass, he and I went instead to the Copenhagen coffee house on the Rathmines Road. I was reading English at Trinity College; and over coffee and ham sandwiches he loved to discuss with me the work of Yeats, Joyce and Beckett. The Copenhagen became his church, where he worshipped at the altar of Anglo-Irish literature.

Jim had a profound respect and admiration for the great writers Dublin has produced; and he nurtured literary ambitions of his own. He naively hoped that if he lived in that word-intoxicated city, some of the Irish linguistic genius would rub off on him. I regarded his innocence with a mixture of impatience and affection; but I did not discourage him.

* * *

The small living-room was the only warm place in the digs, where the borders liked to congregate after supper before going out to their regular watering holes. The room had a fireplace, and the shallow grate contained a heap of damp slack with a few red cracks in it, from which poured thick yellow smoke. On the mantelpiece was a male urinal filled with artificial flowers, flanked by two cheap, loudly-ticking alarm clocks. Above the mantelpiece was a picture of the Sacred Heart, and beside it were three ceramic ducks in flight. A dirty, worn armchair (reserved for Mr. Carmody) and six string seated chairs were arranged around the smokeslack.

The living-room was out of bounds at lunchtimes on Fridays, when the ineffable Sally Noggin graced it with her presence. Jim

* pronounced Neeve

had not been warned of this, and after lunch on his first Friday in the digs, he casually entered the room, and was startled to see Sally stretched out on the hearthrug with her skirt hiked above her hips, uncovering flowered, lace-trimmed knickers of a generous and unflattering cut. She turned on Jim in a fury.

"Git your cock out of here this instant!" she snarled, flinging a gouged loaf of soda bread at his head.

Jim ducked, and hastily shut the door, retreating into the kitchen. Mrs. Carmody gave him a pitying look.

"Isn't she savage? She eats a whole loaf of soda bread with her lunch. And isn't her language straight out of the gutter? Between you and me and the gatepost, I say she's savage."

Before Jim could reply, the kitchen door was wrenched open by Sally Noggin.

"Me little finger's more than what you've got," she raged at Jim. "I'm not fooled by your size, you great fuckin' get. I've been with a few big fellas in me time, and it was always the same: the bigger the keg, the smaller the tap!"

Colour rushed into Jim's face. He gazed at Sally with a kind of awe, as if trying to picture the cesspit of her mind. He made no attempt to defend himself against her slander, but turned his flushed face to Mrs. Carmody with a look of mute appeal.

"Would you dry up, girl," Mrs. Carmody said testily to Sally. "They boy was not to know that you'd be eating your lunch in the living-room instead of sitting at the table with the rest of us."

"I won't have him peepin' up me skirt," fumed Mrs. Noggin. "I'll have the Gardai on to him, so I will."

"Ah for the love of God, would you ever shut your gob, girl," snapped Mrs. Carmody, whose Kerry temper was beginning to ignite. "It's touched in the head you are, I'm telling you. Sure, the boy comes from a home such as you've never seen in your life. And he's as innocent and sheltered as a cleric out at Kimmage. Like a lamb, he is."

"More like a goat to me own way of thinkin'" opined Sally Noggin. "Starin' up me crack like it was a bloody chimney or somethin'."

"Is it outside you want to go, girl?" challenged Mrs. Carmody, the light of the battle in her eyes. "For it's outside you're going, if you don't stop giving out."

"There's no justice in this quare ould world," Mrs. Noggin observed bitterly. "A peace-lovin', God-fearin' Irishwoman can't have a little privacy to ate her small bit of food without bein' gawped at by a fuckin' foreigner, and it's his side you're takin'. But it's the Virgin above watches us down here, and it's for me she's weepin'!"

So saying, Sally Noggin slunk off to the breakfast room to demolish the last of the soda bread.

* * *

Old Mr. Carmody came into the living-room and subsided into the armchair slowly, as if the prepare it by degrees for its load. He reached into his greasy pocket and fished out his blackened pipe, and a bar of equally black plug tobacco. He packed the pipe and held a match to it. As he sucked on the stem, the bowl fumed, the tobacco shreds glowed, and soon pungent clouds of smoke began to poison the room. Mr. Carmody sat back placidly to study Mutt and Jeff in the *Evening Herald*.

I was sitting by the smokeslack reading the *New Statesman*. Tom Neary was catching up on the day's racing news in the evening paper before making his nightly Stations of the Cross -- a crawl to fourteen consecutive pubs.

Mrs. Carmody came in and propped a pair of long coal tongs between the fireplace and the fender. Then she spread two pairs of freshly laundered underpants on the tongs. "Drying out me husband's fart-jackets!" she explained to the company. Then she threw a slice of soda bread on the fire; a few minutes later she retrieved it with a bayonet, and put it on a plate. She settled down in a chair by the fire to nibble the cinder of toast while reading *Butler's Lives of the Saints*.

Tom Neary left to begin his alcoholic odyssey. Mr. Carmody had fallen asleep, his mouth open, gentle snores fluttering his moustache. A cold pipe dangled from one huge limp hand. Mrs. Carmody folded her husband's underpants and put them away in her sewing basket.

I went upstairs to bed. I shared the enormous front room with Rico and Jim. It was a dank, cheerless room, with a bricked-up marble fireplace, and three tall windows that over looked Belgrave Road. A dim light bulb with a dusty paper shade hung from a floral plaster medallion in the centre of the high ceiling. The workmanship was of indifferent quality, and nothing like the magnificent plasterwork to be found in some of Dublin's Georgian houses. The walls were covered with a faded green wallpaper blotched with dark stains of mildew.

Rico had introduced some colour by hanging up posters advertising bullfights in Barcelona and Madrid. He was an aficionado of the matador's dangerous art, and spent the summers attending corridas all over Spain.

When I entered the bedroom, I found that Jim was in bed, and had fallen asleep with the light on. Rico's bed was empty, and I remembered that he was at a party given for him by Trinidadian friends. It was his twenty-first birthday, and a flurry of congratulations and good wishes had awaited him at the breakfast table that morning. Mrs. Carmody had magnanimously served Rico a second boiled egg, to celebrate his coming of age.

I switched off the light, undressed, and climbed into my bed. The sheets were like a river of ice, and it took an hour for me to shiver to sleep.

"Yellow bird, high up in banana tree,
Yellow bird, you sit all alone like me;
Did you lady friend leave de nest again?
Dat is very sad,
Makes me feel so bad;
But you got wings to fly away,
High in de sky away,
You more lucky than me..."

Jim and I were woken by Rico serenading Belgrave Road as he reeled home at a late hour after quaffing an entire bottle of Vat 19 rum at his birthday party.

The unoiled garden gate yawned and clanged as Rico entered the hallowed Carmody precincts and stumbled up the front steps. Singing his wistful ballad, Rico unlocked the front door and groped his way to the stairs. His song ended abruptly in a gurgle of fright. Fergus McFadden, always on the alert for killers, had found one skulking at the foot of the stairs. He seized Rico's throat with one thumbless hand, and with the other rapped him smartly over the head with a poker. Rico screamed and managed to free himself from Mr. McFadden's grip (a lack of thumbs being a definite disadvantage in hand to hand combat). He fled up the stairs to the first landing and locked himself in the bathroom.

Safe inside, he began to sing again. He filled the bath and climbed in fully clothed. His voice trilled through the house:

"Der is a fair city called Dublin,
With cuckolds, muscles, Guinness and gin;
But old Anna Liffey,
She gets pretty niffy
Whenever de tide is not in!"

Rico's song recital was interrupted by the crash of Mr. Carmody's mighty fist on the bathroom door.

"Get up out of that, you drunken blackguard!" he bellowed. "I never heard such a shindy since they shot me brother in the Troubles."

Rico paid no attention. He splashed about in the cold bath and began soaping his suit.

While Fergus McFadden stood guard with his poker, Mr. Carmody went to his tool box and returned with a screwdriver. He began to unscrew the lock on the bathroom door.

A sense of danger percolated through Rico's pickled brain, and he climbed out of the bath. He unlocked the bathroom door and swung it open with a sudden movement. Caught off balance, Mr. Carmody bumped into Mr. McFadden just as the latter was lifting his poker for a lethal blow. The two men crashed to the floor in a tangled, cursing heap, while Rico raced upstairs to our bedroom as nimbly as his sodden clothes would allow.

He peeled off the soaking garments and stood there naked, apparently under the delusion that he was a matador about to enter the bullring for an important corrida. He pulled the sheet off his bed and held it before him like a white muleta.

"Huh! toro!" cried Rico, as he executed a flawless veronica, followed by a series of complex passes. Jim and I watched in silent fascination as Rico disdainfully risked his life against some of Spain's fiercest fighting bulls. He knelt, he danced, he swirled his muleta with a grace and daring which the great Manolete might have envied. Squinting myopically along the blade of his imaginary sword, Rico lunged again and again, dispatching one bull after another with some of the cleanest kills ever seen in Belgrave Road.

Loaded with trophies (six ears and two tails) of his bravery and skill, Rico brought his fiesta brava to a triumphant end. But his brimming bladder informed him that there was another moment of truth to be faced. He flipped open the lid of Jim's paraffin heater and pissed copiously and sibilantly into it. Then he wrapped himself in his muleta and lay down on the floor with his head in the shoe cupboard, imagining that he was stretched out on the warm pink sands of the plaza de toros, receiving (from a somewhat unorthodox position) the acclaim of a wildly cheering crowd.

Jim managed to bundle Rico into bed; a night spent on the frigid floorboards of our bedroom would have given him pneumonia.

The house was quiet again when a volcanic fit of coughing on the front steps announced the homecoming of Mr. Neary, who had arrived with more that the usual number of "jars" aboard. The coughing fit ended with a dreadful hacking, and what sounded like bits of bronchi being spat out.

"Neary my God to Thee!" murmured Jim.

We heard Mr. Neary wheezing painfully as he heaved his bulk up the stairs. There was a calamitous crash. In negotiating the first landing, he had stepped on the screwdriver dropped there by Mr. Carmody when he'd fallen against Mr. McFadden. The walls of Jericho, collapsing to the music of Joshua and his wandering minstrels, could not have made a more impressive impact than did Tom Neary as he landed on the floor.

This time it was Mrs. Carmody who emerged from her bedroom, brandishing a broom.

"Is it the Divil's own ceilidh we're having in this house tonight? Get back on your feet, you fat drunken eejit, and for the love of God, let's have a bit of peace."

She reinforced her request with several hard whacks of the broom on Mr. Neary's adipose anatomy. Jim said she reminded him of Newfoundland seal hunter clubbing a seal pup, except that Mr. Neary look more like a beached whale than a baby seal. Mr. Neary struggled to his feet and lumbered off to his room, and Mrs. Carmody chuntered back to her bed. A few minutes later she gave a scream which might have outshrieked a banshee. Jim and I looked at each other in amazement. Had Mr. Carmody attacked her, demanding his marital rights for the first time in forty years? We looked inquiringly at Rico, who had sobered up a little. He was stuffing the end of his sheet into his mouth to muffle his laughter; tears were running down his dusky face. He explained the reason for Mrs. Carmody's fright.

"O God, mahn! I put some Andrews Liver Salt in de old lady's piss pot. It have a terrific reaction to any kind of acid. When de old lady sit on it and pee, I bet de pot nearly explode, and de bubbles shoot straight up her *cuño*! She ain't gonna forget my birthday, I swear!"

Our bedroom door was flung back on its hinges. Mrs. Carmody stood in the doorway with her trusty broom in one hand. The other held up the skirts of her nightie. A snowy froth of bubbles clung between her wrinkled thighs like a mound of detergent. Cuchulain himself would have quailed at her fury.

A quick glance at the three of us enabled her to identify the desecrator of her chamber pot. She dropped her skirts and grasped the broom handle in a firm two-handed grip. She crossed the room and repeated her imitation of a Newfoundland seal hunter.

"De Gardai gonna have you up for manslaughter!" howled Rico, as he cowered under the blows of the old lady's broom.

"You dirty, stinking -- God forgive me -- animal! What are you after putting in me jerry pot to make it boil over the way it looks like a witch is getting ready to wash out the Divil's fart-jackets?"

"Andrews Liver Salt," confessed Rico.

"Andrews Liver Salt, is it? I'll give you Andrews Liver Salt, you black, good-for-nothing little savage! Coming home stocious, singing at the top of your miserable voice; having a bath in the dead of the night with all your bloody clothes on; throwing me husband down, and himself an old man not able for falls; stripping off your wet clothes and leaving them on the floor in a puddle for the rest of us to mop up, and ... Sacred Heart of Jesus! ...there's another pool under yonder heater! Is it leaking it is, James?"

"It's not the heater that's leaked, Mrs. Carmody," said Jim with a grin.

Comprehension came swiftly to Mrs. Carmody. With her broom flailing, she turned back to the hapless Rico.

"Are you ... are you after *piddling* in it? Oh, Blessed Mother of God! Did you learn nothing at all from the good Irish missionaries in Trinidad?"

Mrs. Carmody gave Rico a final tired clout with her broom and made a weary exit, muttering about darkies that were beyant redemption.

2

When Men Speak That Way

by
Sasenarine Persaud

Winner of the Taliesin Prize for literary criticism, Sasenarine Persaud was born in Guyana in 1958, where he started his writing influenced by the interplay of Judeo-Christian, Islamic, African and Indian cultures. He lives in Scarborough, having immigrated to Canada in 1988. He is the author of two collections of poetry and two novels.

These are of those early mornings on the river. Heaven came to earth for one hour and hell reigned in the following seven - and this is of that time when men speak that way. This was years ago and I had been a junior shipping clerk at the old Bookers Wharf. In those days it had just been renamed the Guyana National Shipping Corporation by the Burnham government, which, firmly entrenched on a "socialist" policy, had nationalized the British Bookers Holdings in the country - the entire sugar industry and the bauxite industry, formerly owned by Americans and the Canadian multinational ALCAN. Business with the metropolitan countries, which supplied all the machinery, even the ships to export the products of these nationalised industries, needless to say, was greatly reduced and unless a boat was alongside and discharging cargo it would be rather quiet at seven a.m., the hour we opened the warehouse for business with the public. Normally it remained quiet until about eight a.m. when the large importers or their agents started calling, enquiring about short-shipped goods, short-landed goods, damaged goods, broached goods...And there were lots of those - broached goods. It was an importer's nightmare and doubly ours - as representing the shippers we were legally responsible for the security of the goods. Legality and law were a joke, yet for "influential" and "connected" people the law could be invoked with a vengeance.

Often, goods transhipped from a European or North American vessel at some Caribbean island port, especially Port-of-Spain in Trinidad and later from Parimaribo in neighbouring Surinam which was suffering from all sorts of shortages because of the 1980 coup, created headaches for us. Goods passing through these ports often arrived broached once these were not sealed in 20' and 40' containers, yet even the containers were no guarantee that cargo would not be broached, and the Guyanese stevedores got all the blame. It was not that the Guyanese stevedores were angels but they were not always the culprits though they did more than their share, unobserved, in the hatches of ships, or while loading or unloading at nights, in the dark hours of the early morning. It was rare to catch them in the act and when caught in the act we on occasion pretended we did not see - the effort of reporting, the investigations of police all very time consuming - and sometimes we felt it was not worth doing. Perhaps we were as corrupt as the stevedors and did not realise it, taking a perverse pleasure in having a hold over them when we knew they knew we saw them stealing and did not report them but it was more because it was an embarrassment to catch them in the act and equally embarrassing to be caught pilfering.

But we knew what they did - everybody knew what they did - even the security at the gate. The stevedors, popularly called the "theifadores" wore huge baggy trousers which easily concealed stolen articles strapped tightly to their legs, calves and thighs. They lived well with the security guards at the check out gate, which meant that the security guards got a percentage of the takings. Greed and especially need, we saw during this era, was the stimulant for acts of the greatest creative originality in dissimulation. Stevedores who were experts at handling the winches and strapping crates to pallets knew exactly which pallets were not quite securely strapped; these were the ones they put down on the wharf just a shade rougher so that crates spilled their scarce, expensive items on the greenheart planks and it took a touch of diabolic genius that would make several spilled items disappear in a trice of time by these phantoms of the docks. All the 'wharfingers' cursed "these black bitches', even the "black" wharfingers. Paid by the hours and in blocks of four hours - four p.m. to eight p.m.; eight p.m. to midnight - they stretched the work at night over midnight, if only by an hour so they could get paid for the entire four hour block...so sleepy and bleary eyed we cursed them all silently at night.

And we cursed them again and again during the day, mainly between eight a.m. to three p.m. as importers or their agents hounded us for their goods - maligned us because their goods were broached.

But that one hour from seven a.m. to eight a.m. when it was so quiet and peaceful made it all bearable. There would be little activity on the wharf, not even from the small ships and trawlers, a few of which would always be docked alongside the wharf. It was not that the occupants of these smaller vessels were not up or had nothing to do, but many of them involved in many shady transactions found it easier, safer to function when the wharf was alive with activity and people and the security and customs were engaged. In that first hour, from our office almost at the top of the huge warehouse, overlooking the majestic Demerara River, we read the newspapers, exchanged ideas, meditated on the frailty of man, the multiplicity of the creator reflected in the River, cursed the government for ruining our country, cursed our people for being so docile and for participating in this destruction of a country once the haven and paradise of the English-speaking West Indies, the prized possession of the western half of the British crown. More often, I would go to my desk overlooking the River and open my ledgers; a sign that I had work to do, was not to be unnecessarily interrupted; a sign that I wanted to be left alone - alone to stare out unto a paradise that no economic ruin, no political and racial discrimination, no blatantly rigged elections could take away from me. I loved to look at the indistinct vegetation on the distant west bank which curved with the river and the flat land along the river bank not unlike the finely pencilled marks women took pride decorating their heads with after having taken off their eyebrows and it would strike me that women's eyebrow liners were a poor imitation. Trees which broke the general line of the distant vegetation did not have to try all manner of artifice to find acceptance in the eye. Every morning once there were no mist or rain on the river I looked for the two tall palm trees, indistinct but recognisable as palms, which stood over all the other trees like the two eyes of god closed over the *Lila*, the play and sport of his creation, the two eyes of god which could open at any moment. It was as though I did not want to miss this opening with its laser gaze.

But if the palms were the eyes, the river was god himself, full, calm, soft as Shiva meditating on *Kailash*. Sometimes it was sugar-brown, rain-muddied, flowing out to the Atlantic with branches, twigs, the fruits of the land, little pieces of gleaned wisdom flowing into the accommodating deluge of the ocean. Sometimes the quiet river lapping at the logs of the wharf before the tide turned sounded like the discourse of Arjuna and Krishna in the face of the two imposing armies about to destroy themselves in the great nuclear battle of the planet earth. Then the river pounded itself and everything else with a ferocity that was simultaneously bitter and sweet and it was as though Shiva had come down from Kailash with fire in his eyes, power, grace, poetry in his feet - the *Nataraja* dancing his eternal and unmatched dance of love, and destruction/creation. Sometimes there would be rain on the river and the other bank, the West bank, would be hidden in the silver wall of water - even ships in midstream would be hidden in the embrace of the falling water - and I would think;
from water to water
from cloud to river
from sea to sky...

and I would feel the urge to write the most beautiful poems in the world, poems as beautiful as Tulsidas', and perhaps I did too when I scribbled lines of poems on unused "blue-books", lines still lying around in old drawers and dusty old cabinets containing documents from other decades, other lives, lines lost in the limbo of time and place. Who knows, perhaps some other junior clerk will come upon them and wonder at the manner of man I were, just as I spent some of those quiet moments looking at old ledgers, wiping away the dust of ages, looking at the handwriting and notes of my predecessors trying to learn something about them, their traits, their souls, their times...One thing gradually dawned on me - and this was that their poetry of numbers left no doubt that they were masters of their pages, spillages were accounted for down to the decimal, ledgers balanced - everything started with and ended with zero. It would remind me of the great Hindu mathematician/philosophers who in their equations of the absolute provided the base of modern civilization.....

That particular morning, Singh had been talking about his past. He was from Better-Hope Village on the East Coast and had worked all his life on the waterfront, at the Guyana National shipping Corporation -GNSC- wharf as it had then become with the advent of nationalisation but he, like most of the older men, always called it "Booka wharf". He was nearing retirement and he was suddenly conscious that he nothing to show for his labour and worse, nothing to expect on his retirement now that there was an "illegal and corrupt" ruling clique. A pension was not certain. The government could decide to "retrench" him just before retirement as they had recently, thousands of other workers (mostly Indians) - thereby not having to pay them pensions. His accumulated savings over the years which would once have made a difference now meant nothing in the face of years of "galloping" inflation since independence - 15 years of it with no end in sight. He was worried but tried to be philosophical about it and passed it off in a bitter-sweet reminiscence of the "good old days" when people cared...The "white" man was strict, but they cared for people, they rewarded a job well done. I had heard it all before but I always listened because although the theme was the same he occasionally remembered a different story to illustrate and support his point. I could never bring myself to tell him that perhaps the "white" man did care - more of his profits than anything else. He knew, after years of ruling people, that the human resource was the greatest resource, his greatest asset in his march to amass wealth. So he had to appear to care - I was tempted to cite him Napoleon and his hand-out of ribbons, worthless ribbons to his soldiers but I could never bring myself to disillusion him further. And maybe he was right. Maybe the "white" men he dealt with did care, even if in a guilt-ridden, condescending way, as much as they were permitted by the monster of a system which had spawned them and I myself, then, could not quite bring myself to believe that some of the people, seeing the wretchedness, perpetuated by a system they administered would be untouched by such wretchedness and exploitation.

I listened to Singh's reminiscences because of the different stories he told to illustrate his various philosophical views. His stories were, for me, a journey back into a time I felt so close to and he told these stories with such attention to detail, such vividness that I used to think that Singh must have been in lives past one of the great Sanskrit sages who orally handed down the knowledge and text of the *Vedas*, the great stories of the *Panchatantra* for centuries without missing a *Shloka*, a word, a pause. When the others were telling stories of the old days and there was any dispute about detail, they all turned to Singh for the correct version - and his word as to the correct version of the event in dispute was accepted without question.

There was a sudden silence that morning and we both looked out unto the quiet river, the crystal clear morning, the billowy white clouds, the clean blue sky, the neatly etched waving of trees on the West Bank - shades of green and suddenly I spoke as I remembered from my past.

"Sometimes it was like this..."

"What?"

"The mornings at South City, when all was quiet..."

"Yes, yu teach there..." he said looking out with me unto the morning river.

"See you later," he said almost inaudibly.

"Yeph," I answered, knowing that he realised that I wanted to be left alone with the memories that were dearest to me and which I had not been willing to let go of yet. But, I went back, hearing the Kiskadees and Blue-Sakies in the tamarind tree, the huge silk-cottons, the wrens in the crumpling steeple of the magnificent, century old Anglican church nearby. During free periods I would go downstairs alone and enjoy that paradise. The wind pattered on the leaves of the trees nearby and the coconut branches like rain in the distance, like the turning tide. That morning it all came back but stuck in my throat and I wasn't ready to talk about it, not yet, I thought, I haven't reached that stage. I turned the newspaper to run away from it and started flipping through the pages. When I saw the announcement, it shocked me. It said simply that Dr. Phillip Shiv Kumar had died quietly in his sleep in New York and had been cremated as was his desire. This numbed me for a while. Life and death were so simple - a few printed words on paper and that was it!

I remembered then all those times I had gone to him - when I was sick and when I wasn't so sick, but wanted leave - a little rest. Abdominal pain, back pain - he would quote the medical terms which I never remembered - and would ask of me, of himself, of the world, somewhat rhetorically; who could dispute that - nobody! "Like the time I was doing exams in Glasgow and they were questioning me..." and he would begin. If there were nobody else, he would sit and talk. He was such a smooth and rivetting talker and I liked to listen to him - the eloquence of his speech - the poetry of his speech in a standard English that was natural and familiar and from which he would slip quickly into a phrase of Hindi-English. Somehow he always seemed to be talking about his years in medical school in Scotland; at least this was where he always began, like in the *Panchatantra* this was his frame story and a narrative would take him to an incident in America, England, Europe, the hinterlands of South America, the holy and unholy places of India - wherever he had travelled. Sometimes there was no moral, or any particular discernable theme in his stories but the telling made them stories, the telling was the essence of the stories - stories without beginning and end, stories in which the stories themselves were plot, theme and moral. And I can picture him now even as I saw him then. He was always so polite and so unruffled that when he spoke about his years in Scotland, or in the remote interior areas he visited as a Government Medical Officer I felt he was not really talking about Scotland or South American outposts, but about a universal truth. I felt at times he looked like Krishna must have looked, calmly delivering the Bhagavata-Gita to Arjuna before the Great Battle, or Mahavira or The Buddha under the Pipal Tree.

It always seemed odd that he never had a nurse or receptionist but would himself some to the door of his office which opened into the waiting room, calling softly, "next", and holding the door open until the patient passed into his office. In a time when Burnham had virtually outlawed the tie in public and official life as a token of the "white man's" colonialism, this man always wore a tie and short-sleeved white or white striped shirt which matched the rim of white hair on his almost bald head.

For several days after I saw his death announcement that morning, I saw him when I looked unto the river and at the indistinct West Bank; old, muscular, short (he was about 5'2') but very neat and tidy, holding the door open. I saw him at his desk talking, and suddenly one morning it dawned on me that one of the reasons I sat so patiently and listened to him was because I knew he was dying. He had given up on life and he knew that I new this and in a way it was like a transmission of the knowledge, orally, from generation to generation before the great

Vedic saints invented grammar and the poetics of written language, before they wrote it all down. I reminded him of his son in New York, whom he wanted to see, he told me that last time I saw him. He on the other hand reminded me of the visions I always had of what I hoped my father would have been like had he not died when I was two, and had I known him. I was his only link to a country he loved so dearly and in which he hoped to see his children grow and blossom. He was my link to a world I had heard and read so much of. He had worked for most of his life in all parts of the country tending the ill because of a dream and a belief in the goodness of man and that dream and belief was broken by the world around him, shattered in the world within. Just before he left for New York, just once, I heard him talk politics.

"Black people can't run a cake-shop! A country" It was the only time I saw a sneer on his face - almost a snarl, the snarl of a cornered, faithful dog, grown old, strong yet, but too wise for its master who must kick it out because its silent wisdom and silent resistance to complete manipulation were unbearable. We said out goodbyes and I took one good look around, and outside in the waiting room too before I went out unto the busy North Road and the haggling of the nearby Bourda Market...

Now my memories float up to my tongue. On the one hand I seem to hear the worldly-wise Niti knowledge of Singh's stories and on the other the Vedanta of Dr. Philip Shiv Kumar expounded in the Panchatantra's mainframe yet beginning-less and endless and then both crossing lines and times and types and forms, merging into each other. I can speak about them now except there is no audience and maybe none is needed as at the time of the beginning of the Sanskrit period - the beginning of the great scribal period of the space we call earth, the end of and beginning of eras, the setting down of the Vedas and Upanishads...Ah but there, there he is as I look up, holding the door open and softly, politely calling:

"Next..."

What more is needed!

3

Carian Wine

by
Lakshmi Gill

*Winner of the Poetry Prize at Western Washington University, USA, Lakshmi Gill's **During Rain, I Plant Chrysanthemums** (1966) is probably the earliest collection of poetry by a South Asian writer in Canada. A "fiercely private" person in her own words, she currently lives with her three children in Vancouver where she teaches.*

Someone ran noiselessly by my door. I leapt up. Was that Sis One? I ran down after her.

"What's going on?"

She looked distraught. "Mama asked me to get Papa. Go back to bed."

Sis Two came down the stairs. We were all in out nightgowns.

"What do you mean--get Papa?"

The house was dark. The servants were in their quarters. We followed her outside. A large full moon, fever yellow, hung low, lighting up the front lawn like an absurd Beckett set. The cool breeze hit us and I felt chilled. We were barefoot. In our haste, we forgot robes and slippers.

On the driveway cement, near the gates, we saw a bulky figure sprawled. There was Papa, dead drunk. He was gazing upwards at the moon. Sis One knelt down beside him and coaxed him to come in.

"It's too cold out here, you'll catch a cold."

He mumbled something about Mama and that he would sleep where he lay.

"You can't do that," Sis One fought back the tears.

We tried moving him but he was too heavy. His legs wouldn't budge.

"What will the servants say?" Sis One urged. "And Mama is waiting for you."

She continued to reason with him, as patiently as she could, though I could see her heart was about to burst in sorrow. How difficult it must be, I thought, to be the eldest. On her shoulders lay all the responsibilities of the name Mama and Papa bore and couldn't bear. She couldn't do anything wrong. She wasn't allowed to. Her marriage would be right and dynastic.

We sat a long time on the cold pavement, trying to think of how to make him get up. He was incoherent but he probably thought he was lucid because he kept on talking. What a headache he was going to have the next day. I looked for him plaintively. This was the man who at the age of 14 had to flee India for Persia while his companions were being rounded up and hanged by the British, who led the exiled Indians to continue the fight for independence, who turned down Nehru's rewards because he said his love for his country was its own reward, this rich poor man, this uncommon common man.

Sis One stood up to, what it seemed to be, bay at the moon, call down the gods, mark the spot. She stood over him like the Italian Baron's sculpture.

The Marochetti angel stood grimly with its arms clasped against its breast, long white wings decidedly stern. Remember Cawnpore. You could say those two words and chills would run down a proper British spine. Not to worry. Sixty two years later, General Dyer managed to double the score, not just to settle it, and throw in some hefty injuries besides. Same victims: women and children. Cawnpore, Amritsar, what did it matter. Hatred runs deep and long like the nourishing sea. Not until swaraj was achieved did the common Hindu see the angel because no one was allowed to enter the compound. Incapable of despotism, or so the claim went, the British in leaving India hurriedly, left these stunning works of art anyway for the despised masses to enjoy, and who remembered Cawnpore now? Art endures but Memory wanes and waxes only when politically expedient. Sixteen hundred and fifty rounds of ammunition, with the superior officer's and the Lt.-Governor of the Punjab's approval. The noble men felt vindicated.

And so the need for vindication grows--the Memorial is immemorial. Soon the entire earth will be covered by white crosses and white angels--the grass pushing against the stone. The Stone over bones.

And he lay there, dead drunk, the impractical philosopher-soldier, the retired freedom fighter, as though freedom didn't have to be won again and again. Like Rizal the Hero in his stone topcoat at the park, he had done his orations and simply let the new generation re-discover the fight in its own way. Well, thanks a lot, Papa. What you secured you must maintain until we are strong enough to maintain it. Revenge, like flotsam waxing in with memory, was stronger than universal Love. It came, it came again, it would come, even the British were still reeling from losing the Raj, they would never recover. In spite of you. A sentimental Fool driven drunk.

"What shall we do? Shall I call Bienvenido?" Sis Two asked.

This was the last resort.

"We could get a blanket and just cover him up here," I suggested.

"And in the morning, when everyone wakes up and sees him? No, we must get him up. Lying here is bad for his health," Sis one insisted.

Not to mention ours in our flimsy cotton. There was not a cloud in the night sky, just this one-eyed Cyclop staring down at us, three thin girls for the gobbling.

"I think he's falling asleep." We would never be able to move him now.

Sis One rubbed his hands. "Papa, papa," she tried to shake him awake.

"I'll get a blanket," I said again.

"Go ask Mama what we should do," Sis two said.

I got up quickly, my legs numb from sitting on the ground at an awkward position. Down the driveway came Bienvenido. He said he was going to check if the gates were locked. He did so and came back to us. We felt foolish but relieved. He seemed to know what was going on. He said he'd call Peping and another houseboy. It took half an hour to get Papa up to his bed, after much heaving, pushing and dragging of the heavy body. I went back to bed, very cold and very sad.

No one woke me up. I woke myself up with a sensation of falling, at 4 p.m.. My throat was parched and I had waves of dizziness and hunger. The house was like Mausolion, Halicarnassos revisited, Mausolos dead drunk upstairs. Romy the bodyguard was at his usual post, waiting. I sat with him. He spoke about his passion for cooking. He described how to cook a dish which reminded me that I was hungry so I called a passing zombie to bring me something to eat. Mona was sitting by the phone, monitoring all the calls, like a radio operator on the field after the battle, wearily, wounded. I found out everyone was out, including me. Romy continued to entertain me with visions of something about crabs with eggs, or was that legs. Such long and involved preparations for a few moments of chewing. We were now both eating young green mango slices with salt which were giving me a stomach ache. I think I'm going to be sick, I told Romy.

"You have to be strong, Jazz," he said. "Like a rock."

Like a stone. I tried this for a few minutes, but I threw up anyway, all over the cerulean Persian carpet, all 640 knots per square inch.

4

Matins

by
Arnold Harrichand Itwaru

Recipient of the Guyana Arts Council Prize for Poetry, Arnold Harrichand Itwaru has a Ph.D. in Sociology and is the author of three books of poetry, two works of fiction, and three critical studies on culture and domination. His forthcoming book, ***Closed Entrances****, looks at aspects of Canadian culture and their relationship with imperialism. A full time writer, he resides in Toronto.*

How sweet the sound of your Name, Lord. Have mercy, have mercy, Lord, I beg of you, have mercy on me, Lord. I don't know what great wrong I've done, but forgive me, have mercy on me, a poor sinner humble before You.

Every day, every year I beg You this, O Merciful One, yet every year You so cruelly test me faith. Why, Lord? O Omniscient Omnipotent Omnipresent One, why? Why has there been all this pain in my small life, Lord God, all this pain, my belov-ed Heavenly Father?

Thou givest and Thou takest. This is what your people always say in each time of death, each painful burial. This is what the pastor always says. And this is all I have, all I know. But I do not wisdom Thou givest and Thou takest.

Six children, You gave me six children in this hard life, Lord, and You took them all from me. One by one, You wrenched them out of my heart before they could talk, before they could walk, year by year. Why, Lord? Why me?

Pain, Lord, too much pain. But I have faith. You know this. You have to. But is all this pain really, as everyone says, as I say, a test of my faith? I have always been faithful, Lord, harsh though your test of me, I have always been faithful.

Year by year my milk soured and soured the gaze of this man I am married to. I did not want to marry, You know this, Lord. I did not want to marry, I did not know what marrying was all about, and I did not want to marry this man. I married this man because Ma wanted me to. And this man till today still thinks it was my fault You took those children, that I killed the fruit of my womb. Lord, must your taking be so harsh, so cruel?

I did not understand many things, but I did not wish the death of my children, I did not want them to die, I did nothing to make them die. No one believes me, and You know all of this, are so far away and ever so silent.

Was I wrong to feel horror in the terribly pain each birth was? This whole thing has been all so painful. I pushed him off me that first night and ran away because I was frightened. I did not know what was happening. I had heard this was what marrying was about, but I did not know I would have been so afraid.

Bear it, mi daughta, bear it, Ma said to me. This was what life was for all the daughters of the world. It was the Divine will, she said. Your will, Lord. I should beg Your forgiveness and ask of you strength to endure, to bear the burden of your will, and I would not find it so hard.

I begged Your forgiveness. I had no intention to go against Your will. I did not intend to sin, I did not think i was sinning when I was so frightened, I begged Your forgiveness, and when he came for me, I went.

But in my heart I did not want to go. I did not like this man whom I was married. He had slapped me that night when I refused to have him have his way with me. I was afraid of him. But I returned to relieve Ma's shame and to do my bounden duty.

But it was horrible, Lord. The burden of Your will was horrible. I have always been afraid of the darkness, You have created, and when he came to me in that strange dark-night bed marrying him had put me on, I was afraid. I did not want him to, but he had his way, and it hurt. It was worse than any of the beatings I received from him many times after.

I still did not understand this, Lord. I do not have the words to really say what happened to me then. It was all against my will, but who am I in the face of Your might and wisdom? Wrested, slapped, torn into, pinned, bleeding, my pain my agony ignored---You did not come to my help. In the darkness of Your night, I was nothing, my Lord. Did you create me for this?

My Lord and Master, my Creator, I wish I hadn't been born. What is my great sin that I suffer so much? Why is it I've known no redemption all my life in this earth of misery where You, my Redeemer, have put me? What is this redemption? How can I know it? Where is it?

Was it wrong for the old people, those I've only heard of, to have ever left India? Was this their sin? Or had they done something long before that, and their punishment was their being fooled and brought here to slave as coolies for the White Man?

Lord, my God, I know Thou art a jealous God, visiting the iniquity of the fathers upon the children unto the third and fourth generation of them that hate Thee. But I have kept Thine commandments, but where if Thine mercy?

Sweet Redeemer, my Lord, my God, I cannot speak for all mothers, but I wanted each child to live so much. I toiled with each child growing in me. I worked together with this man, cutting cane, planting rice, growing and selling things at the roadside market. I worked till I could work no more, and birth forced its pangs in me.

I wanted the children You gave me, Lord, to grow and live, to love and help others live, to have nothing to do with killing. I have never killed another human being. I cannot. I cannot understand how mothers agree to their sons and daughters becoming killers, joining the armies of death everywhere, even when they murder in Your Divine Name.

Buy You took my children, Lord. You left me a pain that has not gone away, will never go away.

Great Giver, Great Receiver, forgive me my sinning this morning in this Your house of worship, and understand my plea. But is Your taking, Lord, not also killing? All around me I see Death drawing away Life, weakening Life, killing Life. This Death You have made. This cruel thing. This horror I am so afraid of.

They blamed me, Lord, for those deaths, my children's. My womb, my breast, my milk, **me** cursed, they said. This man, this husband also. He does not how this hurts. He will never know this, will not understand this, will never be able to.

But do not get me wrong, Lord. This man is not evil. This man is a good man, an honest man. He did not know better when he did whatever he did to me. He thought he was correct and just. It was what the men had always done. It was my woman's lot, my burden in Your Divine and mysterious order, my bounden duty. It was what Life was all about, and I learned to live with it. But I did not like it.

He and I have worked together in sun and rain, labouring barely living, toiling all our lives, and we have come to **this**. We are poor and weak and old and sickly.

Forgive me, Lord, but it is not true that as we sow so shall we reap. Many times, too many times the crops failed, the land dried like bone, thieves stole out cows. This man and I, like the others, planted sugarcane and reaped bitterness. We sowed rive and reaped debts beyond our means. We sowed in hope and this is what we are.

I have toiled on this harsh ground, Your ground, Lord, tilling it, sowing it, taking care of it, trying to live, and now my bones ache, my womb burns, I bleed, my limbs are weak, I grow weaker every day. I am hungry and I have no appetite for eating. But have mercy on me, Lord, have mercy on me this morning in Your Creation.

Is my great sin that I did not want to marry anyone. did not want to marry? I wanted to stay with Ma always. Is this why all this has happened to me, Lord?

I am an old woman, but I am a child of yours, a child to You, a child before Your greatness. I beseech You, Wise One, my Belov-ed Heavenly Father, help me understand. In Your infinite wisdom, You know all of this, but I don't understand much of it.

Forgive me for saying it again and again, but I think of it again and again so many times and I'm no closer to any understanding.

They said I was of the age of marriage, and I had to or else it would have looked bad on Ma, and she had already giver her consent. I married this man I had seen only once before, and he brought me here, but I did not want to come, I did not want to. I was afraid, Lord.

I ran away to Pa's grave and told him I was afraid, I was married and I did not know what was going to happen to me. I was afraid of the stranger I was married to. I did not want to live in a place I did not know. I did not want to live with a man I did not know. I did not.

Before that, every day on my way home from school I used to take the pathway through the burial ground and stop at Pa's grave and talk to him. It was not so painful, to talk to him like that. I felt he could still hear me, although I could not hear him or see him and he could not see me.

You took him away, Lord. You knew best, the priest said. I should not worry, I should not be sad. The Lord giveth and the Lord taketh. The great mystery of Life. But, Lord forgive my saying this, but the priest did not know, he did not know the pain i could speak of, he could not know this.

And how was I not to worry? Pa was not ill. He had his health and strength. He was kind and gentle. And then he was dead. Just like that. Gone. Taken away. Gone forever. Taken away by you, Lord.

All praise to Thee, my Lord God, infinite in wisdom, the Benevolent, the Merciful. Forgive me my sins and give me strength to go on before the light of your day shines no more on me.

One by one they are all gone. Pa, Ma, my brothers, my sister, my children. I do not understand this. Why did they have to go? What has happened to them? Where have they all gone? Will I ever see them again? Will I ever know them again?

I do not understand the pain I knew in each birth I bore before the joy in seeing my child, Your creation---but why this greater pain in each death, Lord? Why this punishment? How could this pleas You, my Lord, my God?

Heavenly Father, Infinite is Thine wisdom, but why must this wisdom create such continuing pain? Must it? And why must the faithful so suffer? Is their lot in life to sing praises to Thee even as they suffer, as I have done, again and again?

There is so much, as I do not remember any more. Sometimes I think of things and they're gone, just like that. They do not come back. The road is so dusty these days, and the bush is growing, I cannot keep it out of the yard.

And it is so hard to get out of bed, and it is becoming harder, but I see You, Lord, walking upon the waters of heaven with outstretched arms, but am I saved?

I know Your body was broken for me, Your blood shed to wash away my sins, but as You know, Lord, I'm not so sure of these things as I once was. That is why I do not take The Sacrament any more.

The last time I took Holy Communion---it seems like only yesterday, Lord---I choked in Your Exalted Presence, You know this, You who know all and everyone, every thought I've thought. It did not feel right although I've taken The Sacrament since I was a girl of twelve.

But I like the sweet voice of the organ each Sunday morning worship hour, the sweet sound of Your Name in the soft moaning of the organ.

I cannot sing You hymns of praise any more, but I praise You all the same. I do not know what has happened to my voice. It is not what it used to be. I do not like to hear it. It does not sound like me. I can no longer sing. I do not talk very often. Besides, what is there to say? What can I say?

I used to hear Your glory in the wind among the trees, Lord, but this too is not what it used to be. The wind and the trees no longer speak to me. I no longer hear them. And I am afraid.

Your hibiscus and oleander have changed colour. They fade every day, even in their full bloom, and there are shadows in the faces of people I know but do not often recognize. I do not know when last I beheld the wonder of Your rainbow, my Lord, my Maker, my sweet Redeemer who liveth forever.

Blessed are they who mourn for they shall be comforted. How sweet this promise, Lord. This is what Your church bells say to me every time they call me to worship, and I have come to pray and worship as often as I could. So much of my life has been mourning, so much, Lord. But I have not been comforted.

The pastor says this comforting will come in my other life with you, Lord, in Your heavenly Kingdom where there are many mansions. I do not know what mansions are, I do not want to live in any, but what about this life here, the only life I know, the only life I have, my little life, Lord?

As you know, Lord, I could no longer bear the blame and the death of my children any more, and I tried to end it all when the last one died. I took that rat poison, but it did not work. I vomited it out and I was sick for weeks after. I never got back the strength I lost, then, and my heart has not stopped burning.

Pray for forgiveness so the Lord will not send you to burn forever in Hell, they told me. And I prayed and begged You, Lord. Have mercy, Lord. My punishment has been long and hard, too hard.

I thanked You, Lord, when the see of death no longer grew in me. I did not want to bear another child, I could not go through another such torment. And, Lord, I never wanted to have children. You know this. I did not know what was happening. I did what I had to. I did not even think of having a child when it all happened. And after the first death I certainly did not want another. Is this why in Your wisdom, Heavenly Father, You took them away?

The seed of death, Lord, the seed of death. That's what in Your infinite wisdom You know I started to think. Have mercy on me, a humble and confused sinner before Your Almighty Throne, Lord. But I have been wondering whether the seed planted in me by this man I am married to was not the seed of death.

I know he wanted a son to carry on his name. He is the last one in his generation begun long ago in that India I have only heard of. He wanted a son. And each child born was a son, each death was a son's death, his son's death, the death of what he most desired. And he blamed me for each sorrow, he blamed me, I was the one who was cursed, I was the evil who bore him what he could not have.

But what about the seed of death, Lord? He had sown his seed in hope, but its fruit did not last. Each time it lived for only a little while, and then it died. I suffered to give it life, but this was not enough. It died. Even in my loving, it died. The seed of death, Lord. Each death taking away something from me, each death killing something in me till I can weep no longer.

I know I'm talking about my children, Lord. The children You gave and took back. Forgive me for thinking like this, but I have no other way. I do not have words like the pastor has, I do not understand much of what the pastor says.

The light has darkened between me and the man I married, this husband of my life, Lord. We do not say much to each other. We have nothing to say. I feel him there in the house we worked so hard to build. He is a shadow near the shadow I am. I do not know what he thinks when like me he stares and stares in silence. But I feel no bitterness.

I feel like going to talk to Pa and Ma at their graves, and I said this to him but he said nothing. Like me his hearing is going and maybe he did not hear me.

Lord, I feel like talking to Pa and Ma, my sister and my brothers once more but the journey is too long, I do not have the strength to make it. I wonder what the place where my navel string is buried is now like. But there is no one there I know any more.

I am afraid, Lord.

This morning before I left the house I looked at him, that shadow, my husband, Lord. We do not look at each other very much, but I looked at him and he looked at me, and Your light, Lord, was so clear. All praise to Thee, my God. The light of Your day was so clear.

I looked at him and he looked at me, Lord. We looked at each other, and I saw for the first time how small and sad and weak and worn and lost he is, Lord. He looked at me at the gate and I told him, I', going, and there was a smile in his eyes.

I am afraid, Lord. I see You walking on the waters of heaven, and I am afraid, Lord.

Have mercy, Lord, have---

The congregation rose to sing, "O Come, O Come, Emanuel" within the soft moaning of the organ, but the old woman was no longer there.

5

The Door I Shut Behind Me

by

Uma Parameswaran

Uma Parameswaran was born in Madras and raised in Nagpur and Jabalpur, India. A Smith-Mundt Fulbright scholar in the U.S., she received her Ph.D. in English Literature from Michigan State University. She currently teaches at the University of Winnipeg. An active member in her community in Winnipeg, she was the founder of PALI (Performing Arts and Literature of India) to organize formal dance instruction, and is the producer of a weekly television show. This story was written in 1967.

The light behind the 'No Smoking-Fasten Seat Belt' sign faded. The trans-Atlantic jetliner tore through dense white clouds into the serene blue of the upper sky. Far below, the clouds thinned out into wisps of cotton candy, and the azure of the sky touched the deeper blue of the ocean on which occasional specks trailed streaks of white. Then there were no more clouds, no more darting streaks, only an unfathomable blue below, above, around.

Chander blinked the glare away and focused his eyes on the book in his hand. The black of the title, the motley orange-yellow-green of the jacket resolved from their hazy halations into a clear spectrum of colours and forms-*The Ramayana,* a new English translation. His mother had given this and Annie Besant's translation of the Bhagavad Gita to him at the airport half-apologetically, half-beseechingly, choosing the last hour so that he would not have the heart to refuse. "Keep it on your table," she had whispered, hastily stepping back lest her heart-throbs spurt out of her eyes. She was an undemonstrative, non-interfering mother, and this was the nearest she had ever come to imposing anything on him. She left it to that single moment and gesture to tell him of her prayers for his safety and her hope that he will turn, occasionally at least, to the wisdom and solace contained in these books.

Chander had made an equally idealistic gesture to himself. On the way to the airport he had stopped the car at a bookstore on Mount Road to get 'some reading matter for the journey' as he sheepishly told his parents; what he had bought was a copy of Chandrasekhar's *Radiative Transfer.* It was not his field of study, nor was it one that would or could be read during a journey. Yet, as the car sped him through his last miles on Indian soil, he had felt an urge to hold that book. To see it was to think of its Indian-born author, and to think of him was to open a world of ambition and inspiration.

"Hullo! I am Kishen Agrawal."

Chander looked up at the unctuous-faced young man who exuded friendliness and perfumed hair oil. He half rose from his seat and took the proffered hand. "V.R. Chander," he said in a low voice though to compensate for the other's crude loudness.

Agrawal sat next to him and started talking about himself. When Chander did not offer corresponding personal details, Agrawal set himself the task of drawing out the information. Chander was annoyed. He disliked the custom of exchanging life stories on sight. However, he was as unaccustomed to evading straight questions as he was to asking them. Reluctantly he submitted to the cross-examination. He was twenty-five years old, had a Ph.D degree from Madras University, was unmarried, had three brothers and two sisters, one of them married. He had a two year research associateship with the University of M. at an annual salary of $8,500.

"Wonderful! You will stay on, of course?"

"Probably."

"You do have an immigrant visa, I suppose. Canadian Immigration gives it to most fellows who come on a salaried job. Unfortunately, being a student, I don't have that passport to lifelong luxury. Have you calculated how much one can save in three years?" He added up various figures-for food, lodging, income tax, insurance, car, entertainment, and the total savings came to a six figure amount in Indian currency.

As the questions and counselling went on Chander was aware of a growing resentment. He also felt acutely self-conscious each time an air hostess or passenger passed by. Agrawal, insensitive to his own loudness and Chander's discomfort, waxed more friendly and voluble. He spoke mostly about his own achievements, but he interspersed his autobiography with adverse comments on western culture. As the air-hostess leaned across to pull out Chander's lunch table he said in Hindi, "Do you see how she sways and leans over? Seductresses all," and he lewdly smacked his lips.

An appetizing aroma of food filled the plane as lunch trays were carried up the aisle. Suddenly Agrawal fell silent, and fidgeted. Chander wondered if he was, perhaps, diffident about the correct use of tableware. Agrawal leaned towards him and asked, "How does the damn flush work?" He jerked his thumb towards the washrooms. Chander wanted to say, "I knew all along that you had a firsthand knowledge of the western way of life." But he softened his sarcasm by saying, "Same as on the other planes."

"On the Delhi-London flight I tried all those knobs and faucets but nothing happened. The handle isn't in its usual place. I am a man of regular habits," he went on piteously, "my whole day is upset if I don't start it right. I am feeling ill already." His face was a study of misery. Feeling mean for having teased him, Chander told him where to look for the pedal. But his sympathy was all too shortlived. When Agrawal returned to his seat it was with the words, "Our toilet habits are much cleaner. These westerners..."

The same trend of criticism was carried through the meal. The westerners were far behind in their culinary arts, they had no taste buds, no appreciation for the finer shades of flavour...

Everything about his neighbour revulsed Chander-his shining rayon suit, his ornate watch strap, his plastered hair, his heavy north Indian accent, his egoism, his shallow generalizations. As Agrawal droned on, Chander has a sense of being trapped, a premonition that it was going to be difficult to shake him off.

The premonition proved correct. When they landed Agrawal took the lead, rather efficiently too. They checked in at a hotel downtown; when Chander came out after a shower he found Agrawal on the bed, busily circling ads concerning inexpensive boarding houses. He had bought both the local newspapers, got a map of the city and information about buses to the university, and weekly guide to the current entertainment programmes in the city.

"How about going to one of these joints after dinner?" he asked, pointing to an illustrated advertisement of a night club. Chander replied that he was not interested. That set Agrawal talking on his favourite topic. It was not yet seven o'clock. Why go to bed so early? And alone too! (Delighted with his joke he repeated it several times.) Surely Chander did not intend turning his back on simple pleasures? Didn't he want to celebrate his arrival? Come on an immigrant visa too! Do in Rome as the Romans do, boy (Again he was tickled by his wit.) "I wish I had your visa! Boy, are you lucky? Let me see your magic wand." He rifled through the contents of Chander's briefcase and extracted the landing card from the passport. He held it as one would a jewel. Theatricalism was part of Agrawal's personality. He declaimed, "...'evidence that the rightful holder is a landed immigrant...' The magic carpet to health, wealth and happiness - THE GREEN CARD!"

Chander dryly said, "It isn't green, it isn't a card, and this isn't the United States."

Agrawal ignored him. "...a treasure to be guarded for ever and aye. Keep it in your wallet." He picked up Chander's wallet and put it in.

Chander stared at the other's thin line of moustache with distaste. Why had he allowed this leech to close in on him? Why had he not parried his questions? walked off to another seat? told him to shut his goddam mouth and go to hell? Was it patience that made him listen to the boor? Was it tolerance that kept him from rebuking? Or was it weakness? Tolerance and weakness-one was considered a virtue, the other a vice, but were they after all different words for the same quality? Was it tolerance that had allowed India to suffer wave after wave of political and cultural invasions? Tolerance that had prompted Hinduism to be so submissive while missionaries and governments had drawn away its people and wealth? Or was it weakness? Non-violence or cowardice? Two nomenclatures for the same quality, and that quality a national trait for a people who flaunted it by using the more flattering name...a nation made of spineless thinkers and unthinking egotists...and the Agrawals always led the Chanders by the nose...because the Chanders permitted them to...

Agrawal was saying, "You ask it, we have it. That is the way the wind blows here. And the peaches you can't get for money you can get with sweet words as you will see on campus..."

Chander stood over the other man's bed. Words stormed their way out, virulent, devastating words. Agrawal was a bundle of preconceptions and prejudices, a shallow, selfish, callow brute, pampered by his illiterate society which adulated university graduates as gods on earth. What a society! Gossipy women who at thirty were already elephantine, with pendulous breasts and flabby abdomens, lazy debauched men relaxing the afternoons away against dirty bolsters in they fly-infested shops, chewing betel leaves and spitting tobacco juice on the sidewalks below their shops, selling adulterated sweetmeats and shortweight grocery to poor customers whom they further exploited with usurious loans...

Chander stopped, shocked, when Agrawal burst into sobs. Agrawal defiantly spluttered between sobs, "I *am* a shopkeeper's son. My mother *is* a gossip, and my wife is fat. My children do play on the street with snotty noses. But I love them, I want them. I would rather have them around me, and me on my ropestrung cot in my dung-polished courtyard than be this...here..." he flailed his hands helplessly against the newspaper sheets that crumpled and rustled under him.

Chander's shocked distaste changed to fascination as he watched the prone figure on the bed crying unashamedly. It dawned on him that he envied this man. He envied him for this experience, this feeling of utter lostness in new surroundings, this surging, tempestuous, irrational onslaught of nostalgia for persons and a place. This man could live a life of discovery because he could be carried away by wonder, could be moved to tears by yearnings. In Chander there was no yearning, there was no wonder at the sight and feel of a civilization so different from his own. At that moment Chander forgave Agrawal for everything realizing that some subconscious feeling of lostness had moved him into attaching himself to a fellow countryman.

"I'd give anything in the world to see one of my own people, to hear my own language," Agrawal was saying. With a shock of short-circuited sympathy Chander realized that Agrawal was not talking of his family, but of his linguistic community. Here they were, two men who came from the same country, saluted the same flag, worshipped the same gods, yet so alien to each other! Was the alienness due to individual differences alone? "My own people, my own language..." Could they never be one people unless they had but one language? Was it, after all, only language that could hold a nation together in peacetime?

Be that as it may, this man needed to see his own people, and to speak his own language. An idea struck him. He reached out for the telephone directory.

"Maybe we could run through a list of names common in your part of the country," he said.

Agrawal jumped up. "Great idea! Let's do that." He unceremoniously grabbed the directory and flipped through the pages spelling out the names aloud. "No, no Agrawal, or Agrawal, no Panday or Pande or Pandya...Shrivastava, here is one, Shrivastava, Manohar K. Sunset2-6309, what is that, Sunset?"

Chander explained, and Agrawal went to the phone. The ensuing conversation was loud and cheerful at both ends of the line, Shrivastava was just starting out for the Mundhras' home; they had an informal get-together of Indians on the first Saturday of every month, Agrawal and his friend were most welcome, he would come by in ten minutes and pick them up; hadn't they dined yet? they'd get used to early dinners in this country...no matter, Mrs. Mundhra will surely have something...

Agrawal was excited. He plastered down his hair and reknotted his tie. He scooped his clothes from his suitcase and pulled out a stack of phonograph records from the bottom. He pulled out a bag of small packets. "I must take these. Betel leaves are to us as LSD is to Ginsberg eh? There are dehydrated and powdered, isn't that great?" He emptied more than half the contents into his coat pockets.

"That's a lot to take," Chander said.

"Poor guys, they haven't tasted it in years, I bet."

Chander felt a twinge of guilt. He had brought two pounds of scented and spiced areca nuts, but he did not want to share it with anyone. Suddenly he knew what he envied in Agrawal. Spontaneity. That was it. Spontaneous nostalgia, fellow-feeling, generosity.

At the Mundhras' Agrawal greeted everyone with warm enthusiasm. Chander could not. As always, he shrank into himself in company. He had always attributed the withdrawal to sensitivity, but now, still in the mood of reassessing values, he accused himself of innate snobbishness. I am the insensitive one, he reflected, a clod that cannot respond or be touched by any strong emotion.

Mrs. Mundhra, a smiling, sweetfaced woman with several rungs of fat showing at the waist, served them a meal of sorts. Then they joined the twenty odd persons in the large living room. Chander, somewhat thawed out of his aloofness, was handed over from person to person, all of whom asked the same questions about his work and gave the same assurances on the friendliness of the people and related the same jokes about the winter ahead.

Within minutes Agrawal had become part of the company. Chander had noted that he did not use his native Hindi very long. There were people from different parts of India, and everyone spoke only English. Even the children who came in from the adjoining room spoke English. At first Chander instinctively shied away from the twang and accent in the children's speech; he was being absurd, he told himself, as the interpreter at the embassy in France who resigned his job because even the local children spoke better French than he did. Rationalising did not assuage the hurt that Chander felt at being told that the children spoke no other language. The lady he questioned replied, "...my baby's first words were in our Marathi-Aai Dada-but once I started taking her out to the park it became "Mommy-Daddy", and now she doesn't even understand Marathi."

A man next to her said, "Just you wait a few years and she will be correcting your English! My ten-year-old daughter is on tenterhooks whenever her friends drop in; she is afraid we'll say or do something wrong."

They spoke with complacent pride.

In India Indians built walls of "My people, my language' between themselves. Here Indians apparently could not care less whether their children had any knowledge or feeling about their country, religion and language. Slowly the implication of their immigrant status dawned on him. Till now he had thought of his visa only as an unwanted and tedious formality, a wasteful trip to Delhi for a personal interview at the High Commission which had lasted less than ten minutes, and had consisted solely of questions that he had already answered on the printed forms. Now, he gathered from others' experiences that it was a precious document that many of their acquaintances had not succeeded in obtaining. They narrated the stories with the smugness of people who had 'arrived' talking sympathetically of those who had not made it.

With increasing bewilderment and hurt Chander noted their attitudes.

Someone asked him if conditions in India were really bad. Conversation stopped and everyone waited for his reply. Just as he started telling them about the drought, one of the women chipped in to tell him in detail about the thousand dollars they had collected last year for the soldiers. She spoke in a gushy manner of 'the girls who worked so hard', and of the dinner and folk dances they had arranged. Chander was annoyed that the Indo-Chinese war should have been no more to her than an occasion for a social venture. But the others seemed to enjoy her loquaciousness. Chander then spoke of the long queues everywhere, for grain, fuel, milk, medicine...He realized that his audience was being politely sympathetic, as though he was sharing some personal grief which was outside their orbits of interest. Roused to anger by their callous indifference, Chander continued in a higher key of emotion. He spoke of the blackmarketing, the rampant corruption and bribery and inefficiency...He was conscious that he was magnifying their indifference and exaggerating his descriptions, but he felt impelled to provoke them into active sympathy and identification. They were not provoked. They politely changed the topic; once again conversation groups were formed, and Chander found himself in a group that was sorting out Agrawal's records.

"Do you have any Pankaj Mullick records?" someone asked.

Agrawal did not. Another asked for classical recordings. Agrawal drew a blank there too. He had all the latest film hits but no one seemed interested.

"Ah! here is a Saigal album," a young man enthusiastically brandished the record. Several others responded, and in silence everyone heard the first song. Then they spoke of old films. Saigal sang on in the background. There was deep nostalgia in the air.

What astounded Chander was that they spoke of the distant past. The first among them to leave India had left it only ten years ago, yet the India they had in mind was not the India they had left but the India of their boyhood, and often enough not even that. The young man who was jubilant at finding the Saigal album could not have heard or seen Saigal on the silver screen because Saigal was out of the 1940's; so that what he recalled was not even his actual boyhood but the dreams of his boyhood. To some of them trams still trundled by on Madras streets, anti-British slogans and processions still rang through the country, and Lala Amarnath's double century against Don Bradman's eleven was still the greatest event in cricket history.

It was not callous indifference that prompted them to be blind and deaf; it was some nostalgic idealism, or was it escapism? They seemed to have an image in mind, a golden age of romanticised memories. They did not even want to experience those pleasures again as was evident when Agrawal passed a plate of his betel packets. They reminisced about the betel-areca shops at the street corners, the vendor dipping into a dozen different tins of spices and liquids to make up the roll of stuffed betel leaf, the roadside Romeos clustered round his little shop..., but only a few took Agrawal's packets.

What were they? Indians or Canadians? They had not changed their food habits; the women had not changed their costume; apparently they were a close-knit ethnic group; still far from being assimilated into the general current of life around them. Yet they were as far from the Indian current. They shied away from talk of their return. They hoped to go back, they said, but Chander felt that their hope was for a time as far in the abstract future as their memory was for an abstract past.

Like the mythological king, Trishanku, they stood suspended between two worlds, unable to enter either, and making a heaven of their own.

Chander felt a great weight within himself. "This smoke-music-voice filled air has given me a headache," he told himself, moving to a corner table and picking up a deck of cards. Mechanically he started a game of solitaire.

But the weight was not in his head. It was in his chest, a thudding, throbbing weight. The throbbing stopped but the weight remained, and also an inexplicable sense of loss, anger and contempt.

Chandler pulled out his wallet and looked at the light blue piece of paper on the top left corner of which a crown floated above a shield held by a lion and a unicorn. "This card is required for customs clearance and when making application for citizenship. It will also prove useful for many other purposes." He looked at the words as though they held a threat. The passport to lifelong luxury...the devil's bait to lifelong exile...

He sat very still, staring at the words. He felt a great surge inside him, a swirling, forceful torrent sweeping onwards and dashing furiously against the sluice gates of self-control. For a moment he indulged in the thought of what a relief it would be to let himself be carried away in that current. But years of emotional restraint held their own. "I am distorting things - people and values -out of all proportion; I am being irrational, childish, making an emotional furore over a harmless piece of document, two inches by eight, that holds no more compulsion or threat than my driver's license portends death in an accident." Even so, he could not bring himself to replace that card in his wallet. He was aware that someone was approaching the table. Quickly he continued his game of solitaire. A pale, short man of thirty-five pulled a chair and joined him.

"That is enthralling music," he said, "the album got into Agrawal's collection by mistake, one would think." His voice was surprisingly rich for his small body, and his fingers surprisingly long and slender. Chander watched him beat to the rhythm of the record on the table.

"You read characters fast," Chander said, relaxing.

"He wears his on his sleeve. A bore, but goodhearted. This album must be a recent addition. I thought I had all of Ravi Shankar's recordings."

"This is his latest. Came out a few months ago."

"Beautiful! It is so different from his other records. The sitar is a sad-sounding instrument and Ravi Shankar...just listen to what the maestro does with it! You can almost hear the anklet bells of dancing women! So different from his usual pathos!"

The music built up towards a crescendo of joy. He continued to soliloquise, "We are a happy people, an innocent people. Our devotional songs are love songs because our god is our lover, not our judge. We do not crawl on our knees to his throne, we dance our way into his arms. We were not meant to suffer and starve. Nor to exploit and deprave each other."

Chander felt a happy kinship with this man. He extended his hand and said, "By the way, I didn't get your name. Mine is Chander."

"I am Harish Bahl."

"Glad to know you. Your name was mentioned earlier, I forgot in what connection. Oh yes...er..." Chander's grip loosened instinctively as he remembered.

"Married to a Canadian," Bahl completed gently, withdrawing his hand.

Chander was acutely conscious of the weight again. It was right there, inert, crushing.

Once: Chander was fourteen. It was his first season in an adult cricket team. His eldest brother, Adityan, was the captain. It was the final day in the final match of the tournament. Chander returned to the pavilion after forty minutes of steady batting and twenty-two runs. At three o'clock he had to go home and accompany his grandmother to the temple. When he left the field they needed thirty-five runs to win the match and the trophy. Thirty-five runs to make in ninety minutes with four wickets in hand. It was as easy as eating jam.

But when he returned home at half past five, the boy next door hollered to him that they had lost, "thanks to the captain scooping a ball right into the bowler's hands" ten minutes after Chander had left. The other wickets had fallen like ninepins of course.

Chander had run into the house and to his brother's room. In blind anger and disappointment he rushed at his brother, intending to hit him with all his might. But the closed fist did not smite. They fell limply on the older boy's chest and he burst out crying. He buried his face against his brother's shirt where the sweat had made a yellow half-moon under the armpit and he sobbed. That was the last time Chander had cried actual tears. He felt those tears rising again, tears from the depth of some divine despair rising for the second time that evening. But he was not fourteen now, and Bahl was not his brother. Yet, for a moment, hearing that rich voice he had thought, seeing those ascetic eyes he had hoped, holding that firm clasp he had felt...Chander sat very still and stared at the half-finished game of solitaire.

Bahl picked up an issue of 'Time' from a side-table and sat down across from him. Though all Chander wanted was to be by himself, he felt self-conscious, constrained to say something. There was always that inane but safe loophole, the weather. "So warm in here, one wouldn't know it is close to freezing outside," he said.

"The first winter is usually quite enjoyable, every day a challenge; it is the second or third winter that gets one down."

"I don't expect to be here that long. I just want to pick up some work-experience and go back home."

"That's what we all say for the first year or two. And then it's too late. One more brain-drain casualty." His eyes moved to Chander's landing card.

That's all right. We can do without you and your like, Chander wanted to hit at him. But at the same time he felt accused and impelled to defend himself. "This is the age of individualism," he said, "and not of abstract ideologies of patriotism and nation-building."

"Absolutely," Bahl said quietly, again more to the open magazine in his hand than to Chander. His voice was like the murmur of breeze on water. "I alone am important, not abstract ideologies of patriotism and nation-building, go piss them away down the rivulets cascading down the Nilgiris where the eucalyptus leaves crackling underfoot spark boyish fancies that flame like the sun's glorious spurt of blood before it sinks behind the blue hills where wafts the smell of coffeeshrubs between which slither silent cobras that raise their hoods to the piper's tune as he puffs his cheeks and contorts his wiry frame at Sulluru station to entertain into coin-throwing the Grand Trunk passengers going north through teaktigerdacoit jungles and the plain where the Ganga flows from the mountains where Himavan rules and Siva dances on snowbound Kailas the dance of joy from which alone doth spring love laughter every worthwhile thing...and I metamorphose into a hybrid way of life ostrichwise ignore the bonds that break one by one, and grow grey with renown and riches, and children who will never know their lost patrimony or knowing, hold it in contempt."

In the silence that followed, the sounds of the plaintive sitar picked up again, and from the farther recesses and rooms came the buzz of conversation. More briskly Bahl said, "When we leave our country we shut many doors behind us though we are not aware of it at the time."

Chander willing his hands into steadiness, carefully placed the queen of hearts below the king of spades and said, "There are many doors ahead of us."

6

A Tin of Cookies

by
M G Vassanji

Writer-in-Residence at the University of Iowa in its prestigious International Writing Program for Fall 1989, Moyez Vassanji was born in Kenya and raised in Tanzania. Thus he brings a firsthand experience of the South Asian experience in an African context, the basis of his first novel, The Gunny Sack, which won the Regional Commonwealth Prize for a first novel. Before coming to Canada in 1978, he attended the MIT in Massachusetts, and the University of Pennsylvania where he earned his doctorate in Physics. He is also the author of No New Land, *a novel,* Uhuru Street, *a collection of stories, and a children's drama* The Ghost of Bagamoyo. *He lives in Toronto with his wife and two sons.*

When she realized she was awake, it was with a nagging thought. Perhaps it came in the wake of a dream, she wasn't quite sure. It would not be easy to go back to sleep now. She was a worrier, and spending sleepless nights was nothing new to her. She had done it as far back as she could remember. Nevertheless she changed positions and tried to relax, pretending the thought away. She tried going to sleep on her back, drawing up one knee and crooking one leg sideways, but then immediately went back on her side: she never slept on her back. She put a pillow on her head, her ear, and thought of her little grandson in Red Deer, Alberta. A happy thought, but it did not stay. The real, the nagging thought was: what if she died that night?

She was a woman of sixty-five, who drew comfort from her beliefs. The thought of death itself therefore did not frighten but came quite naturally. Her mother had died at sixty-five, or an age as close to that as far as anyone had ascertained. At her age, like many others, she awaited if not actually anticipated death. She had raised her children and educated them well. And when her husband was living, in her youth, the two of them helped as many poor relations as came their way. This had been her religion, her dharma. Now that she really had no one--her children lead their own lives and related to her only out of duty or charity--it only remained for her to accomplish more dharma in whatever time she had left. In bed she had taken to singing hymns to herself, and she woke up every night in the quiet pre-dawn hour to meditate. She had taken to visiting her relatives--brothers and sisters and in-laws: not an easy feat, this, considering the distances to which they had dispersed. All this in preparation for death, her departure. She never knew, when she said good-bye, if it was for the last time.

It was the thought of the kind of image she would leave behind her after she left that now worried her as she tried to get back to sleep.

There was not a sound in the house. She was given the room to herself, her grandniece having volunteered to sleep on the floor downstairs. The girl could have slept on the sofa, but she preferred the floor, as many kids would for excitement's sake. Outside, the wind whistled past the open window, and the clothesline rattled. From a distance came the sounds of cars zipping along the highway. She had often wondered about these sounds. All these people. Going here and going there...rushing around...Where could they all be going? She rather preferred the quiet of Red Deer, and looked forward to returning.

It was the end of summer. Two weeks remained of her two-month visit to Toronto; the next day her son would come to fetch her. Finally. Lately she had begun to wonder if he had not neglected her. She had spent six weeks shuttling between her niece, her friend Gula, and her brother, while Jameel had been busy with one trip then another, then with other guests and moving houses. Now he was free. The thought that he had managed to avoid her caused in her a pain sharp enough to penetrate all her defences, her excuses for him. Did he feel that she would be lured by his comfortable lifestyle into staying for good? Her pain was all the more sharp for the thought had indeed crossed her mind...that she might be happier here...and he had guessed. She sometimes tested him, feeling the ground as it were, to see how welcome she was. She had told him once that after she died she wanted to be born in his home, so he could educate her and make her smart. "I'm not ready for kids yet, Ma," he had said. To which she had promptly replied, "And I'm not ready to go as yet, I too have a little time," and he'd been quite embarrassed.

She had already packed for her visit. She had put all that she would need for the next two weeks in a handbag and two plastic shopping bags. The rest of her things she had put away in her large suitcase, which she did not plan to open until she went back to Alberta. In the handbag she had tucked a sweater she had bought for Jameel's wife from Honest Ed's with the price tag carefully removed. It was a nice, thick sweater with buttons, a light blue design on a cream-coloured background. She had picked it after a lot of hesitation. Her friend Gula had like it. But she was too embarrassed to show it around in this house: her choice would invariably get the laughs. When you don't bring them anything they taunt you and call you stingy ("Now where will you take your money?")--and when you bring something carefully selected, they turn up their noses in scorn. They had become so high and mighty with their education and their English...and who had slaved all day in those smelly stores in Africa selling chilli and spice to put them here?

The expedition to Honest Ed's and back had taken Gula and herself close to five hours. In their broken English and with the boldness that each other's company gave them they managed to buy all they wanted. At the end of the trip Gula had given her a present: a packet of home made toast and cookies. "For your son. This will put him in a good mood." They had become like two schoolgirls. Funny, she thought, not to have had a close friend in forty years, and now--after all this water under the bridge--to have found one. They had parted gravely, Gula to her son, and she waiting for hers to come.

Gula's package was now under the sweater in the handbag, and with it was a box of imported cookies she had bought from Honest Ed's at a bargain. These goodies, gifts for her son and his wife, who she believed did not have the time to make such delicacies at home--or to buy them cheaply--now preoccupied her mind in the middle of the night and refused to budge. What, she worried, if she died that night?--then her niece would discover them in the morning, and what would she think? That Auntie could not spare even a cookie for her children; did not have even the decency to share the delicacies she had brought--not only that, but she hadn't even had the grace to show around in the house the presents her friend had given her--and like a thief in the night had tucked them away in her bag (under the sweater) while no one was present or looking. And the truth was that there were so many sweets in this house that no one looked at them twice. The kids did not eat home-made sweets and even at the sight of a curry on the dining table their faces would fall, and they would chew their way grudgingly through the food. Once she had brought home a cake, and it had stayed uneaten, she herself feeling too shy to finish off something she had brought for others, until it had rotted and had to be thrown away. And not that she didn't treat them otherwise. She did what she could. During Eid she gave five dollars each to the kids, until she began to wonder if it had really been worth it coming to Toronto. All the allowances she received from her sons spent on kids who didn't need money and forgot about it the moment they turned their backs on you, because they received so much more from elsewhere.

She made a sudden decision. She sat up in bed, her feet dangling at the side, and thought about it. She would take the tin of cookies out of the handbag and put it on the kitchen table. In the morning she would tell them it was a treat from her. It had slipped her mind, she would imply, until she came across it again while rearranging her things. At breakfast they would eat the cookies; and in the future they would remember that.

Light from the street below illuminated the room and she could see the shapes of various objects in front of her. The door was shut, and pants hung on it from hooks. To the right was a desk on which were strewn some clothes, and between the door and the desk lay an old metal bathroom scale that no one had the heart to throw out. This house is like a souk, she thought, a market. To the far left, in the corner was a box that she knew contained old clothes, waiting for an as yet unknown charity.

She struggled out of bed, a little unsteady on her feet. She waited for some moments, bending forward a little, her hands pointed unwittingly to her arthritic knees and ready to clutch them the moment an undue pain shot through them. It did not come, and she started toward the door. She stepped on a pair of socks as she opened it and went into the landing. A low snore reverberated in the half darkness. Against the railing stood an exercise bicycle, at the sight of which she pulled a face. Three bicycles in the hallway downstairs, and this metallic idiot upstairs. As she thought this her foot struck on one of the extremities of the thing and she stubbed a toe. She chocked back a scream, but a muffled grunt escaped her throat. For a while she stood there, completely still. Framed in the nightlight in the landing, feeling every throb pulsating her toe, waiting for the agony to pass. Her lips were pressed together and her eyes were moist; she hoped she hadn't been heard. I must be patient, she thought, I must collect myself or I will never make it down the stairs...and serve me right. When she was little she believed that the moment you spoke ill of someone, you invariably brought a small misfortune upon yourself. Like an instant punishment. You could bite your tongue that way; or stub your toe, or land a foot in a puddle. That way a greater calamity was avoided.

The two doors on her left were shut and the one on her right was ajar, from which the light drone of the snore escaped. When the pain dulled she took the few paces to the stairs and started to go down. She took one step at a time and paused every few steps for a breath. The house was new, and the stairs did not creak. Half way down there was a mirror, at which she glanced. She saw a dark, featureless shape, but she knew she must look like a witch. Her dentures were soaking in a yogurt container upstairs, and her hair, without her hairpiece, looked thin and scraggly and oily.

At the foot of the stairs was a heap of shoes belonging to the family; and to a side, near the bicycles and under the stairs, were her suitcase and handbag. She bent painfully over the handbag, unzipped it, and started rummaging in it for the tin of cookies, creating a slight rustle of wrapping papers as she did so. Almost near the end of her efforts a doubt came upon her, and she paused. Perhaps she should leave it there, she thought. Morning would soon be upon them. But then-- The thought that had escaped her in her struggles down the stairs returned. What if--? For such a small thing she would be remembered as a mean and selfish old woman. Who remembers the charities of our youth? And she fished out the tin, making a final rustle, and took it to the kitchen. A little out of breath, she put it on the table. She thought she should take a peek at the contents, and she pulled out a chair, making only the slightest squeak, sat down on it, and tried to peel off the tape that sealed the lid. She failed, and got up to fetch a knife. As she started shuffling to the drawers, the front of her slipper caught at the edge of the kitchen rug and she fell on it with a thud. The tin of cookies rolled away from her hand.

Complete silence returned, for a moment. Then there was a sound in the living room. She tried to get up, muttering to herself. The main light went on and her tall teenage grandniece, Sharmila, lumbered in. "What are you doing, Mami?" Without waiting for an answer she helped the old woman to the chair. Then she gave her a drink of water and rephrased her question. Meanwhile there was commotion upstairs. Doors opening, exclamations, the toilet flushing. The rest of the family trooped downstairs. Her niece Almas, followed by her two sons and husband.

She was embarrassed and hard put for explanations. Her back was hurting, and her hands hurt from having taken the fall. Her toe still throbbed. She felt depressed. The tin of cookies was detected against the edge of the kitchen door, where it had come trundling to a stop. She found that no explanations were needed. The mood was one of relief and humour, and the exclamations expressed concern.

"Mami, you'll hurt yourself this way. Couldn't you wait till morning?"

"Well, if she's hungry what should she do..."

"Yes, she doesn't eat at night. I'll make some tea! Who would like some tea?"

"This tin hasn't been opened yet. I'll bring one that's open." It was put away.

And, for some reason she didn't quite know, she started to laugh, and she laughed until there were tears in her eyes.

7

Calabogie

by
Cyril Dabydeen

Poet Laureate of the City of Ottawa from 1984 to 1987, Cyril was born in Guyana and has been in Canada since 1970. Writing poetry (7 collections), short fiction (2 collections) and novels (2), editing anthologies (2) and serving as a critic and essayist, he is truly 'a straddler of the genres'. With an MA in English and a Master of Public Aministration: both from Queen's University, Kingston, he currently teaches Creative Writing at the University of Ottawa and serves as a Race Relations specialist with municipalities and the federal government. Featured in several creative and critical journals, in Canada and abroad, his contributions have earned him a place in the **Canadian Who's Who.** *He currently lives in Ottawa, Ontario.*

The girls kept throwing the bluish-pink slipper into the shallow neck of the winding lake where the water gurgled, spouted, and occasionally hissed. At this angle from where we were the lake was more a rivulet, dwarfed almost by the high promontory of a cliff fifty yards to the left from which divers, one after the other, catapulted themselves. Below, along the banks on both sides, rocks jutted out in serrated formation, some with slippery green moss treacherously carpeting them. To the far right about one hundred yards away, a nude male bather leisurely basked on a flat whale of stone, indifferent to the loud din created by the two slim thirteen-year-old girls; the bather seemed indifferent to us as well.

"Be careful--gosh!" shrieked one of the girls, long-limbed, bespectacled. The other, more sprightly and precocious-looking, laughed in the sun, teeth glistering as she commenced a balancing act across the narrow platform rafting the portion of water close to her. Now and again she looked at the divers, vague as they seemed, almost unreal; and they too were looking at her as she remained poised, her left leg raised--indicating an exquisite curve of thigh tapering to the instep. The afternoon sun glistened everywhere, not least on the cliff-divers with an aura of peace; only the playful cries from the girls shattered the quiet, the bespectacled one directing the other to the slipper as it tugged against a large rock. From time to time the girls glanced at the nude bather who seemed in his early twenties, their shrieks suddenly becoming insistent. The entire spot no longer appeared covert or the monopoly of the one bather; now it echoed with a benign hostility as the girls shrieked louder. The nude bather, as far as we could tell, shifted from his reclining position and looked more studiedly at the girls trying to retrieve the slipper. Suddenly the girls appeared tense.

Laura, lying next to me on her side, a white-spotted greenish bikini with a tongue of strap poised on her navel, blonde hair spangled in strands reaching to her ribs, also looked at the slipper as the current pulled against the rock. The girls seemed even more tense as the slipper remained stationary. Laura muttered that it needed nudging before it could get into the running stream again. The shapely body of the one precocious girl, Sue, became steadily arched, poised; the other, Jill, with agitation kept on urging her to get on with it: to reach out and grab the slipper!

Laura lifted her shoulder, neck, to get a better view. So did I, close to her; while the nude bather now appeared to stand up, then sat down again, remaining still as pumice in the August sun, a shimmer and haze everywhere; the cliff divers again catapulting themselves into the unfathomable depths, as if lost forever.

The delicate wrist of one hand moved forward, almost pulsing in the sunlight. "Go on, get it!" cried the bespectacled girl. But the slipper was held by the resinous moss, evading the outstretched hand; and just when it was on the verge of becoming free, it seemed held again by a tangle of moss about to distil the slipper's pink-and-blue coloration. A further surge of water, the current pulling in one direction, the slipper with a tail of moss in another.

"She won't get it," Laura said, breaking into a dim smile.

"Maybe," I replied.

"No."

"She will," I suddenly stiffened.

The nude bather rose, sat down again; he smiled in the sun, his body's outline now more than a silhouette, well formed as he was; and he seemed now less indifferent to us: no longer in a world of his own. Laura looked away from him to the slipper and the girls, though the hand still stretched out, fingers like tendrils reaching further. Then my attention shifted to Laura, her well-shaped back, taut muscles curving close to the lower spine and glazing in the sun. "She won't get it," Laura repeated.

The girl with the glasses shrieked raucously, like a seagull that was lost and was now finding its way back with others. The other girl, Sue, rangier now, kept leaning forward as far as she could, her entire body stretching, almost about to touch the slipper.

I caressed Laura's shoulder, wondering why we really came here: why she chose this spot. "It'd be private," she said, on our first real date. Maybe she wanted us to be far away from everyone else in the city; and maybe now we'd really get to know each other better: we'd talk about things we didn't previously say despite a vague shyness, discomfort. But once more came the intrusive sound of the divers, thwarting our expectation in a way; another diver screaming as he floated in air, then finally hitting the water. The next, a woman in her early twenties, hefty despite her silhouetted form, lifted her arms, body taut in the sun as she flew in! "You know, it's amazing how they do it," Laura said. "Yes," I muttered, following the diver's plunge.

"They're good at it too." Laura said, turning to my side, an almost questioning look in her eyes. "I mean those two." She pointed to the thirteen-year-olds who were still trying to retrieve the slipper: their determination now above all else; and the nude bather fidgeted, as if he no longer felt comfortable being part of stone, rock, or landscape. But my attention was rivetted once again to the slipper, the water tugging harder, the moss itself pulling it. The girl with glasses, Jill, took her turn now, grit etching her mouth, eyes suddenly smaller behind the glasses as she tentatively moved forward, stepping upon the next rock, and the next. "I am scared," she blurted out, freckles suddenly iridescent behind the grey glasses.

"You mustn't be, Jill," said the precocious one, turning in the direction of the whale of stone, the nude bather like pumice still in the distance.

"I can't help it!"

"Gosh!" came the sharp response.

Laura chuckled and quickly seemed even more attractive: it was all a part of her manner in this seeming wilderness with more rocks, trees; the weather perfect, lulling us. The next diver on the cliff, a strong, wiry-looking youth with curly hair: a trained gymnast, he seemed, spinning in the air before hitting the water with an almost reluctant splash. I heard the one girl closer to us say: "Get my slipper. It's mine!"

"I can't," cried Jill. "It's too far away."

"You must; it's your turn!"

"I am trying; but I'm scared!"

The moss, as if in the air; the next diver, circling the water. The nude bather, still basking, slowly getting up.

"It was you who threw it in!"

"No, you!"

"You did, deliberately."

"No!"

"Yes!"

Their caterwauling, defying me to drowse; then, like incantation: "Get my slipper!"

"I can't!"

"GET IT!"

Suddenly, loud pitched raucous laughter: the precocious one glancing in the distance to the nude one's silhouetted form, her hair thrown back, mouth, lips pursed. Jill, as if always bespectacled, raged on:

"It was you! You can't deny it; you threw it in, Sue!"

They argued, laughed; again stepping onto more slippery rock and moss moving with the current, filaments of grass. My eyes closed, dreaming in a way; the nude bather looming larger, shifting with the clouds close to the cliff-divers.

"Don't deny it!" one girl shrieked.

Laura merely watched me--I could tell--and smiled, caught up in the girls' playful frenzy. Opening my eyes, I looked into the water: at how black it suddenly was, a dim movement. Shadows, the clouds drifting, darkening. A further amorphousness not far from the girls' feet against a ledge of stone, moss, as I started thinking how earlier Laura and I had glided along the water: and I, reluctant, suddenly cartwheeled into it, unable to maintain my grip. Laura thoroughly laughed at that. I swam behind amidst sudden eddying whorls, long hair golden against her skin's tapestry as we moved closer to where the cliff-divers kept coming in like suicidal lemmings. An hour of floating, paddling: my own selfconsciousness in a way; and we sometimes hailed the divers from afar, perfect strangers as we were but held by a common bond as if by the trees, rocks: all our silent moments, reverie, then intermittent splash. The next diver coming in; and we looked up in dread, awe.

Lying still in the occasional silence, I figured Laura was thinking of her ex-husband, Perry: he, in the Saint John with their two-year-old Meaghan: the latter was spending the summer with him. Laura was absolutely devoted to Meaghan, thinking about her daughter's safety all the time. And what did Meaghan talk about with her father? About whom she was now seeing?

"It's your fault!"

"No...yours!"

"The slipper, you must get it! It's mine!"

"No, mine!"

My eyes were now glued to one spot in the water before us where the two thirteen-year-olds stood and then frantically waved. More amorphousness, something moving, clambering with invisible, yet palpable arms; a distinct shape. Laura, so silent, as if she'd drifted away--no longer by my side in the seemingly wayward sun. Then she stirred; she too was looking fixedly at the one spot. Had she seen it?

Almost three in the afternoon, it was; but suddenly time seemed irrelevant. Nothing else mattered in the consistency of weather, like glue; the world itself now indecipherable with water, stone, sky, the lake's widening perimeter. The nudist standing up in the angle of sun, his expression one of strange intensity. A crow floating about, skirting the trees, branches, the whirring air; the slipper moving sideways! The precocious girl, Sue, her wrist throbbing as she once more leaned forward: it'd be her last attempt, her hand shaking as she concentrated harder. Jill urged: "Go on, you will get it now!"

There were no snakes here, I thought; the rock formation, the crevices, holes in the ground, underwater. Something still moving...NO! A prehistoric semblance, or elongated form that once was a part of stone carpeting the moss: with eyes, mouth, teeth, a distinct head. It kept moving towards Sue with a deliberate intent; her wrist still throbbing.

I turned to Laura.

But she was smiling, Laura, in her own impenetrable guise; still thinking about Meaghan? The watery object blended with the environment akin to a diorama, unreal--yet real. An odd rhythm too, the object moving slowly towards the outstretched hand.

I rubbed my eyes, harder.

The girl's hand pulled back in an instant, as water gurgled.

"It's so amazing," muttered Laura.

"What is?"

"The kids--what they can do. What they're up to! Their parents, diving maybe. When I was their age, I wasn't ever allowed to be alone." She yawned.

I concentrated on the moving object, eyes, teeth; moss, greenish-yellowish. Both girls now looking directly at the nude one as he started walking toward them in the afternoon air. Instinctively they blushed, one lowering her head. Silence in the midst of the nudist's strides--he bent on proclaiming the area as his own. Another crow hiccupped and moved blackly against the disc of sun, swirling in the direction where the divers were, the lake mirroring the cliff as if with a distant eye; the horizon itself seeming to move forward. Yet I kept studying the formation--like an obsession--searching for a clue to explain it as it seemed removed from all else: the sky, divers, depths far below. Another diver coming in!

The snake, or whatever it was, seemed to derive from the moss: things unseen, yet were simultaneously palpable, creeping out of rock and sediment, gliding forward, but really wasn't.

The one girls's outstretched hand, Sue's delicate fingers, wrist; my throat dry. Laura stiffened. She saw it too!

I searched the reptile for a mouth, flap of ears, a semblance of what it really was, and wasn't; other appendages; gills; a tongue whipping out. Laura merely looked at me, with an odd questioning expression, her entire body tense, every fibre animated yet simultaneously congealed. In a further angle of sun, another diver loomed, face an odd, twisted grotesquerie as he began somersaulting, then finally landing in the water with unexpected precision.

"You alright?" Laura asked.

I didn't answer. But I kept looking at her, as if she was the one who wasn't well. I figured the nude bather was now walking deliberately towards us, as one of the girls let out a wild whoop --in total disarray; Sue, it was, more precocious now with long curly hair, her shrill cries in the air amidst the birds' somersault, the sun's wild glister and haze. More divers coming in all at once, as if in a further collective drowning. And that snake--it alone--curling and uncurling in the water; a commotion really. *Let's run away*, I heard: a mute tongue's expression.

"Come on, Jill!" called out the other.

"Let's first get the slipper, Sue!"

"It's too late. It's not mine!"

"You said it was yours!"

"No!"

"It's not mine either!"

Their laughter, this game; the nude one still resolutely coming forward, the sun itself now a slab of rock or shale.

Jill started crying, sobbing. And Sue, well, she lamented--looking at us for help maybe, as the bather kept coming; then she too started sobbing. And the current surged at their feet, their bending down at once as if their lives depended on it, all of the lake, water.

Laura quickly stretched out a hand towards me, managing a smile; but now we were both looking at the nude bather, hoping he would stop. . .maybe he was just an illusion ofthe sun and sky, or a distinct shadow. Maybe. My eyes fell upon the water again, but the girls' melodramatic cries, sobs, seemed now to frighten off whatever it was--which was no longer there! That object, serpentine in a way amidst the rock, moss, was now translucent. Lurking...the nude bather advancing.

"Come on, let's hurry!" cried Sue, in mock desperation.

"Yes, we must!"

"No, let's stay some more; that slipper!"

"We must hurry!"

"What for?" Sue's accusing, harsh eye "I can't run barefooted!"

"Yes-you-can!"

"I can't!"

"You-can-so!"

Laura muttered: "Children nowadays, these girls, they're a far cry from when I was growing up." She'd said this before; and she looked at the nude bather claiming his spot, territoriality in a way; the deliberate strides he took in the unabashed air. Laura added: "You see, it's for real. Maybe it's just fun these days. Life for them is, I mean." She looked around wistfully, and maybe again she was thinking of Meaghan. "Soon, they will grow out of it--maybe."

I didn't reply; as I once more looked into the water: looked at every iota of jetsam, flotsam, moss, weed; and I kept imagining a hand reaching out, a frail wrist; fingers' tremors; the slipper itself close by. The nude bather was just a hundred yards from us; he'd paced himself well, and now he stopped, tentative, not sure what to do next, almost hovering. The two girls suddenly started running--away--hopping across rocks, stones. It was all they could do, it seemed. Then Sue turned around, as if to have a last look at him: no other, nothing else; and she screamed hard once more, and then sobbed. But in no time the girls were sprinting ahead again, leaping like fauns, their constantly urging each other on, to *hurry up*!

I watched them ascend the cliff amidst bramble, rhododendron, sage brush; to be with the others: parents, sisters, brothers, whoever. Laura watched them too, as if expecting another collective dive, a daring somersault in the air. It was the two girls' turn now maybe. The air rose about us. A *swoosh*. Laura, well, she held her breath. The nude one, standing there, also looking at the girls high up about fifty yards away; maybe they could see us better--see everything better as they lifted their arms, then started to flutter, ready to fly, slim bodies etched against a bland sky. Breasts, hips, thighs, waist; I waited for the familiar shrieks, a primal scream--whatever--before they hurled themselves down!

The air kept them still; the sound or silence, a mute voice; the girls still flying in a way: the air's wings, bodies floating in the gauze of sun, all the eddying currents below; the nude bather, astride a rock, steadfast; crows' ascent. Applause from the others...down, down. I looked into the vortex of pool, lake, invisible stars in the middle, below. I waited for them to surface; Laura's hand in mine, fingers tightening.

Why then I began looking again for the amorphous form, I didn't know. Then I thought I saw it: moss with eyes, teeth, mouth; an appendage, ears, a chest that curved, underbelly: a stomach propped against a small ledge of rock; a tail swishing with hair like ends, protuberance. Laura's hand still in mine, tightening...Would they ever surface--those two? I kept thinking of the lake swallowing them forever. No! I imagined their wet faces, and so lovely they looked while leaping off the cliff...And where was the slipper? The nude bather, close by...he was retrieving it, with a strong hand, fingers pointed; glancing sideways at the cliff, then into the water...and maybe he'd lift the slipper in the air like a trophy just when the girls surfaced, diaphanously, clad with ringlets of water...out of foam no less!

Again I thought of Laura and I in the water earlier, her gold-spangled body, hair: so lovely she looked, attractive. And why was I with her and no other? Our uncommon origins: she white, and I--markedly different, with distinctly brown complexion. Our longing and expectation again amidst trees, rock, here in this semi-wilderness spot we also thought was ours! "We should be getting back now," Laura quietly said. "It's getting late."

Our hands intertwined, with vague tension, surprise and yet expectancy. Will they ever rise up--those two, remaining so interminably long at the bottom?

Suddenly I began thinking about Laura and I now on the cliff: and our future lives depended on it, hands tightly held, clutched; as we started diving off, sailing in air: our mammoth breath; eyes looking down to the very centre--the far bottom--where moss subsisted on moss; stone on stone. And right then I saw the two girls, hair streaming against their faces at the far bottom; arms and legs working; lungs at full capacity, eyes closed, cheeks puffed!

But in a sense I was really on hard ground, Laura still close to me. And suddenly I was looking again for the nude bather with slipper in hand.

But he was no longer there; he seemed to have vanished in the sun. Did he? And I imagined the girls rising up in a swoosh, so quickly, their heads puncturing the formidably placid surface of the lake. And those ones on the cliff, the adults, all started a rhapsodic applause; as if they were really applauding us--Laura and me. Jill and Sue were also applauding; as if in a way telling us that their game with the slipper was for us; no other. Our fate was tied to it!

Louder, the sounds: against the crows' formation.

Above, below, the thing unseen, yet seen. An object no less, more palpable, in the mind or imagination, swirling--and yet being fully at rest!

8

Mirage in the Cave

by
Surjeet Kalsey

An Associate Editor of the Toronto South Asian Review, Surjeet was born in the Punjab, and was a newscaster for All India Radio before coming to Canada in 1974. She has 2 collections of poetry in English and a third forthcoming, and one in Punjabi. With a Master's Degree in Creative Writing from the University of British Columbia, scriptwriting is her latest interest. Active in the community, she was Coordinator of the 1991 Punjabi Literary Forum in Vancouver, and is also a member of Samaanta (equality), a non-profit group to eradicate violence against women and children in the community. Married to Ajmer Rode, a dramatist and poet, and mother of a daughter and son, she lives in Richmond, BC.

The door slid open, red and blue waters were gushing in the four compartments-as if two glasses were full of red wine and two with blueberry juice. What was it? She couldn't recall a thing. What was floating on the gushing red and blue waters-perhaps the corpses of the past memories. What memories? Did she have any memory chamber left in her brain? What she felt now was just a dark blue slate-a blank rock devoid of any imprint. Her name was perhaps Sirjana. She had lived with a man called Mokshdev, who used to pass every moment in the state of forgetting and couldn't recall things that happened even an hour ago. Mokshdev often used to talk to her as if he saw her for the first time. Sometimes, he would act according to the expressions on Sirjana's face: if she was sad, he had to be sad; if she was angry so was he. What was it, what happened? What could be anticipated to fill the blanks? What was missing? Even she didn't know.

Mokshdev had gone far from her life, perhaps forever, leaving her alone. The loneliness drew her towards the door of those red and blue compartments and she walked downstairs within. Passing through the zigzag and dark tunnels, filled with stink of dead flowers and rotten leaves, she entered some unknown place, where only the trees stood dry and withered with their roots in the scorching sand. A moment later, instead of the trees, she saw bodies of men, whose skin looked burnt like the stale peeled apples laid bare in the scorching sun. Their flesh shining with perspiration, their eyes wide open towards the blank sky, they were craving for rain drops. The clouds did sometimes overcast the sky, but soon they would turn into burning fire and begin to scatter in sparks, each spark, giving birth to a desire that wandered in the deserts, and died by scorching or by committing suicide before its fulfilment.

The men whose skin looked like stale peeled apples began to melt, changing their form and evolving into a new species. This process made possible the appearance of a few women too; consequently, the men stopped melting. On seeing the female bodies, the males of the new species snatched from the trees a wild parasitical vine, two inches thick and hundred feet long. They cut it with their teeth to make whips, and lashed the female bodies till the red brown whip marks swelled out on their backs. Suddenly leaving this animal act, they ran towards a smokey building, and threw themselves against its crumbling wall. Sirjana, terrified by the happenings, began to feel her body with her fingertips, softly, so she might not hurt the bruises. She knew that for ages women had bruises on the bodies, yet they had risen from the dirt, with no tears, no fears, no sighs, and no complaints. They came with hands full of edibles, and gave them to those high headed creatures, who snatched everything like hungry wolves and devoured. After filling their stomachs to their full, their eyes became more red, more full of sheen. The women thought, the men were still hungry, and they began to cut their limbs one by one for them; some snatched flesh from their thighs and calves, and some from even their hearts and livers. When the women turned to mere skeletons the men felt as if they were contented. The men found themselves laughing, singing and dancing madly. In no time, however, they realized that they were still hungry-their passions rose, starving. But how would these skeletons satisfy them now? The thought shocked them, and helplessly they began to repent. Soon it struck them that they should plant those female skeletons in the earth (like trees that already stood bare, devoid of leaves), when the spring would come these skeletons might get their flesh back. And they planted the female skeletons in the sand.

It was almost midnight; a dreadful silence spread around. Sirjana tried to sleep under her blanket. Her mind by traversing the tangled pages of history, was driving her mad. There were damp caves; sometimes a glow-worm streaked its tiny light in the dark. She heard weeping and wailing of women; perhaps they were still alive. But this noise was coming from the other side of the void. Sirjana stressed her eyes and saw, in the purple dim light a young beautiful woman tied to a pole with chains; some middle and some old aged women were battering her mercilessly. What was her fault? What crime had she committed? Sirjana began to tremble at the scene...Then in the purple dim light there appeared a face of a handsome young man whose body too was tied with chains. She thought there must be some ethical dispute or violation of moral standards like the taking of freedom by young folks or disobeying the by-laws of ethics. Sirjana wondered and got confused. This might be an incident of good old days, who knows? It might be the time when the round curves did not even evolve on earth, when woman was brave, when she reigned over the passions of man - husband, son, brother. (And the man she conceived had to become her owner one day.) What was that civilization from Volga to Ganges? Wonderful or shameful?

In the meantime, a tall strongly built middle aged woman appeared, and she untied the young man from the tree. She kissed the brow and putting her arm in his arm, she walked leading all the rest of the females; singing and laughing they disappeared into a thick dark purple haze. Only the girl tied in chains was left behind.

Intending to free the girl, Sirjana walked towards her, but the closer she came to the girl the more the girl began to disappear. In the end, she could see, in the place of the girl, only a skeleton

- it was only a painting of the skeleton. To make sure, she again touched the painting - yes, this was the true picture of some lost civilization when woman was the Chief or General. What made woman so vulnerable afterwards? Nobody knows.

No night, no daylight. What was this piece of earth devoid of a sky - a lost life in some gutter perhaps. It was hard to understand - was this a search for the self or non-self? Who was her's in the remains of these caves of the sub-consciousness - the caves - damp, stingy and dark with an indifferent attitude towards her. Things lost their meanings in the swamp of time, although there might be some truth underneath - a truth of the body and a truth of unseen consciousness.

She had no idea how much night was gone, and how much was ahead; only the violent lights and deep purple lights were left behind; flashing in front of her eyes were the yellow sick lights, in which the face of woman seemed sickly and pulled long. In this colony a man was marching with a woman, instead of shoes, on his feet. When he walked with his heavy body, the shoes shrieked and bit his feet. When he rebuked and threatened her life if she dared to argue, she didn't seal her lips. Her only fault was that she resisted and refused to be 'the shoes' forever.

It was one o'clock in the morning and she wasn't sure what she meant by losing him. She knew she won't let him sift like sand through her life, nor would her heritage allow her to do so. "A woman is a woman after all, and she should remain under her veil," argue some philosophers. Shutting her eyes, she pulled the blanket on her face, and started scanning those lines she once wrote to him: We did have some relationship, I don't know what to call it. Relationships have no meaning without feelings, do they? I suppose not. We live like blocks, bricks or machines. We expanded our matter and our properties indeed, and neither of us tried to win the war of custody of our expanded flesh and blood. We were merely programmed to stay under one roof, and on lonely cold beds - so many nights, so many years walked away unquenched sand...being loved by someone is more than anything in this world...what a feeling, what a thirst for self-realization...

Suddenly, she uncovered her face and threw the blankets aside. Her arm hit the flower vase; it fell, the glass shattering on the floor. Her mind was running over mad thoughts - where had all the people gone? Where were they now? Yes, the loneliness could squeeze feelings out of her like a lemon, it could never devour her. It only dissected her brain and unseamed the memories of him again and again. She began to wander in the unknown unseen ruins, underneath which countless faces were smashed, crushed, and disfigured in the lost civilization. These faces still agitate when the wind blows, they convulse with the pain when the lava breaks out, man's finger bones holding woman's finger bones crack down, countless fossils of jaws laugh hysterically.

He was no longer with her, but deep down in her heart she felt his existence still lingered on. What if she hadn't lost him completely - grief, frustration, dejection? - no, nothing could touch her now. Don't we lose things in life, and sometimes precious ones, too? For a moment she stared at the broken shards of the vase. Her eyes didn't move but her lips projected a smile, and slowly, shutting the windows of her eyes, she pulled the blanket over her face again.

9

Lend Me Your Light

by
Rohinton Mistry

Winner of the 1991 Governor-General's Award for the novel, Such a Long Journey, *Rohinton Mistry was born in Bombay, India in 1952. He immigrated to Canada in 1975, and began writing in 1983 as a student at the University of Toronto. His talents earned early recognition when he won two Hart House literary prizes, and later Canadian Fiction Magazine's annual Contributor's Prize. His first collection of stories was titled* Tales from Firozsha Baag. *He is presently working on his second novel.*

We both left Bombay the same year. He first, for New York, then I, for Toronto. As immigrants in North America, our sharing of this common experience should have salvaged something from our acquaintanceship. It went back such a long way, to our school days.

To sustain an acquaintanceship does not take very much. A friendship, that's another thing. Strange, then, that it has ended so completely, and I will probably never meet him again.

Jamshed was really my brother's friend. The three of us went to the same school. Jamshed and my brother Percy, both four years older than I, were in the same class. They had to part company during lunch, though, because Jamshed did not eat where Percy and I did, in the school's drillhall-cum-lunchroom.

To this drillhall were delivered lunches from homes all over the city. The tiffin carriers would stagger into the school compound with their long, narrow rickety crates balanced on their heads, each carrying fifty tiffin boxes. When these boxes were unpacked, the drillhall would be filled with a smell that is hard to forget, thick as swill, as the aroma of four hundred separate steaming lunches started to mingle. The smell must have soaked into the very walls and ceiling. No matter what the hour of the day, that hot, crowded grotto of a drillhall smelled stale and sickly, the way a vomit-splashed room does after the vomit is cleaned up.

Jamshed did not eat in this crammed and cavernous interior. He did not breathe the air redolent of vomit-lunch odours. His food arrived precisely at one o'clock in the chauffeur-driven, air-conditioned family car, and was eaten in the leather-upholstered luxury of the back seat.

In this snug dining room where chauffeur double as waiter, Jamshed lunched through his school days, safe from the vicissitudes of climate. The monsoon may drench the tiffin carries to the bone and turn cold the lunch boxes of four hundred waiting schoolboys, but it did not touch Jamshed or his lunch. The tiffin carriers may arrive glistening and stinking of sweat in the hot season, with scorching hot tiffin boxes, hotter than they'd left the kitchen of Bombay, but Jamshed's lunch remained unaffected.

During these school years, my brother Percy spent many weekend afternoons at his friend's house. When he returned, our mother would commence the questioning: What did they eat? Was Jamshed's mother home? What did the two of them do all afternoon? Did they go out anywhere? And so on.

Since my brother did not confide in me very much in those days, these interrogations were the only way I could satisfy my curiosity about Percy and Jamshed. I found that the afternoons were usually spent making model airplanes and listening to music. The airplanes were simple gliders in the early years, and the music was mainly Mantovani and from Broadway shows. Later came more complex models with gasoline engines and remote control, and classical music from Bach to Poulenc.

The model airplanes and records were all gifts from Jamshed's numerous and itinerant aunts and uncles, purchased during business trips to England or the U.S. Everyone except my brother and I seemed to have aunts and uncles smitten by wanderlust, and Jamshed's supply line from the Western world guaranteed for him a steady diet of foreign clothes, shoes and records.

One Saturday, Percy reported during question period that Jamshed had just received the original soundtrack of My Fair Lady. This was sensational news. The LP was not available in Bombay, and a few privately imported or "smuggled" copies, brought in by people like Jamshed's relatives, were selling in the black market for two hundred rupees. I had seen the records displayed side by side with foreign perfumes, chocolates, and cheeses at the pavement stalls of "smugglers" along Flora Fountain.

After strenuous negotiations in which mother, Percy, and I exhausted ourselves, he agreed to ask his friend if I could come and listen to the album. Arrangements were made, and next Saturday we set off for Jamshed's house. Jamshed welcomed me graciously and put the record on the turntable.

The afternoon went by slowly once the soundtrack had been played. I watched them work on an airplane; then we had lunch and talked. We talked of school, the school library, all the books that the library badly needed: and we talked of the "ghatis" who were flooding the school of late.

Ghatis were always flooding places, they never just went there, in the particular version of reality which we inherited. Ghatis were flooding the banks, desecrating the sanctity of institutions, and taking up all the coveted jobs. Ghatis were even flooding the colleges and universities, a thing unheard of. Wherever you turned, ghatis were flooding the place.

With much shame I remember this word ghati. A suppurating sore of a word, oozing the stench of bigotry. It consigned a whole race to the mute roles of coolies and menials, forever unredeemable.

Once, as a child, I watched with detachment while a straining coolie loaded our family's baggage on his person during one of our rare vacations to Matheran. The big metal trunk he carried flat on his head, with the leather suitcase over it. The enormous hold-all he slung by its strap on his left arm, raised this arm to steady the load on his head, and picked up the remaining suitcase with his right hand. This skeletal man, like an underfed, overworked beast of burden then tottered off, toward the train that would transport us to the little hill station. There, other human beasts of burden would be waiting with rickshaws.

Automobiles were prohibited in Matheran, to preserve the pastoral purity of the place.

Many years later, I found myself at the same hill station, a member of my college hikers' club, labouring up its slope with a knapsack. Automobiles were still not permitted in Matheran, and every time a rickshaw sped by, we'd yell at the occupant: "Capitalist pig! Stop riding on your brother's back, you bastard!" The bewildered passenger would lean forward for a moment, not quite understanding, then fall back into the cushioned comfort of the rickshaw.

But this kind of smug socialism did not come till much later. First we had to reckon with school uniforms, brown paper covers for textbooks and exercise books, and the mad morning rush for the school bus. I remember how Percy used to rage and shout at the scrawny ghaton if the pathetic creature ever got in his way as she swept and mopped the floors. Our mother would proudly observe, "He has a temper just like Grandpa's." She would also discreetly admonish Percy, since this was in the days when it was becoming difficult to find new ghatons, especially if the first one quit due to abuse from the scion of the family and established her reasons for quitting among her colleagues. The good old days, when you could scream at a ghaton that you would kick her and hurl her down the stairs, and yet expect her to show up for work the next morning, had definitely passed.

After high school, Percy and Jamshed went to different colleges, and if they met at all, it would be at concerts of the Bombay Chamber Orchestra. My brother had stopped yelling at ghatons by this time. With a group of college friends he organized a charitable agency that collected and distributed funds to destitute farmers in a small Maharashtrian village. The idea was to get as many of these wretched souls as possible out of the clutches of the village moneylenders.

Jamshed showed a very superficial interest in Percy's activities, and every time they met, he would start with how he was trying his best to get out of the country. "There is absolutely no future in this stupid country," he would say. "Corruption is all over the place. You cannot but any of the things you want, you don't even get to see a decent English movie. The first chance I get I'm going to settle abroad, preferably in the U.S."

Jamshed did manage to leave. He came one day to say goodbye to Percy, but Percy was away working in his small village. He and his friends had taken on the task full time.

Jamshed spoke to those of us who were at home, and we heartily agreed that he was doing the right thing. There just weren't any prospects in this country.

My parents proudly announced that I, too, was trying to emigrate, but to Toronto, and not New York. "We will miss him if he gets to go," they told Jamshed, "but for the sake of his own future, he must. There is a lot of opportunity in Toronto. We've even seen advertisements in newspapers from England, where Canadian Immigration is encouraging people to go to Canada. Of course, they will not advertise in a country like India - who would want those bloody ghatis to come charging into their land? - but the office in New Delhi is holding interviews and accepting highly qualified applicants." According to my parents I would have no difficulty being selected, what with my education and Westernized background. And they were right. A few months later, things were ready for my departure to Toronto.

But as I slept on my last night in Bombay, a searing pain in my eyes, like something out of a Greek tragedy, woke me up. it was one o'clock, so I bathed my eyes and tried to get back to sleep. Half-jokingly, I saw myself on trial, guilty of hubris in deciding to emigrate, paying the price in burnt-out eyes: I Tiresias, blind and throbbing between two lives, the one in Bombay, and the one to come in Toronto.

In the morning, the doctor said it was conjunctivitis, nothing very serious, but I would need some drops in my eyes every four hours and protective dark glasses till the infection was gone.

And so my last day in Bombay, the city of all my days till then, was spent behind dark glasses. The glimpses of my bed, my desk, my cricket bat, the chest of drawers I used to share with Percy, came through dark glasses; the neighbourhood I grew up in, with the chemist's store ("Open Twenty-four Hours"), the Irani restaurant, the sugarcane-juice vendor, the fruit-and-vegetable stall, all of these I surveyed through dark glasses; the huddle of relatives at the airport, by the final barrier through which only ticket holders could pass, I waved to and saw one last time through dark glasses.

Tense with excitement I walked across the tarmac, slightly chilled by the gusting winds, or so I convinced myself. Then, eyes red with conjunctivitis, pocket bulging with the ridiculously large bottle of eye drops, and mind confused by a thousand half-formed thoughts and doubts, I boarded the aircraft.

After almost a year in Toronto, I received a letter from Jamshed, from New York - a very neat missive, with an elegant little label showing his name and address. He wrote that he'd been to Bombay the previous month because in every letter his mother had been pestering him to visit: "While there, I went to see your folks, and was happy that you were successful in leaving India, but was disappointed that Percy was still not interested. I cannot understand what it is that keeps him in that dismal place. All his efforts to help the farmers will be in vain, nothing will ever change. There is just too much corruption. It is all part of the ghati mentality. I offered to help Percy to immigrate if he ever changes his mind, because I have developed a lot of contacts in New York," and on and on; finally: "Bombay is horrible. It seems dirtier than ever, and the whole thing just made me sick. I had my fill of it in two weeks and was glad to leave." He ended with an invitation to New York.

What I read was only the kind of stuff I would have expected in a letter from Jamshed. Still, it irritated me. It was puzzling that he could express so much disdain and discontent even when he was no longer living under those conditions. Was it himself he was angry at, for not being able to come to terms with matters as Percy had? Was it because of the powerlessness that all of us experience who, mistaking weakness for strength, walk away from one thing or another?

I sat down and started a most punctilious reply to his letter. Very properly, I thanked him for visiting my parents and for his concern about Percy. Equally properly, I reciprocated his invitation to New York with one to Toronto. Then, like a sly warlock adding an ingredient to his cauldron not called for in the recipe, I wrote a detailed description of the segment of Gerrard Street in Toronto known as Little India. I promised that when he visited, we would go to all the little restaurants there and gorge ourselves with bhel-puri, pani-puri, batata-wada, kulfi, as authentic as any in Bombay; then, we could stop by the shops selling imported items like spices and Hindi records, and maybe even catch a Hindi movie at the Naaz Cinema. I often went to Little India, I wrote; he would be certain to have a great time.

The truth is, I have been there just once, and on that occasion I fled the place within a very short time, feeling extremely ill at ease and ashamed of myself, wondering why all this did not make me feel homesick or at least a little nostalgic. But Jamshed did not have to know any of it, and my letter must have told him that whatever he suffered from, I did not share. For a long time after this, I did not hear from him.

My days were always full. I attended evening classes at the University of Toronto, desultorily gathering philosophy credits, and worked during the day. I became a member of the Zoroastrian Society of Ontario. Hoping to meet people from Bombay, I also went to their Parsi New Year celebrations and dinner.

The event was held at a community centre rented for the occasion and, as the evening progressed, took on at an alarming rate the semblance and ethos of a wedding party at Cama Baug in Bombay as we Parsis talked at the top of our voices, embraced heartily, drank heartily, and ate heartily. It was Cama Baug refurbished and modernized, Cama Baug without the cluster of beggars by the entrance gate, who waited for the feasting to end so that they could come in and claim the garbage cans.

My membership in the Society led to dinner invitations at the homes of Parsis. The guests at these gatherings were not the type who would be regulars in Little India, but who would go there with the air of tourists, pretending to discover what they had always lived with.

These were people who knew all about the different airlines that flew to Bombay; they were the virtuosi of transatlantic travel. If someone inquired of the most recent traveller, "How was your trip to India?" another would be ready to ask, "What airline did you fly?" Once this favourite topic was introduced, the evening would resemble a convention of travel agents expounding on the salient features of their preferred airlines.

After a few such copiously educational evenings, I knew what the odds were of my baggage being lost if I travelled airline A; the best food was served on airline B; departures were always delayed with airline C (the company had a ghati sense of time and punctuality, they said); the washrooms were filthy and blocked up on airline D (no fault of airline D, they explained, it was the low class of public that travelled on it).

Of Bombay itself the conversation was restricted to the shopping they'd done. They brought back tales of villainous shopkeepers who tried to cheat them because they could sense that here was the affluence of foreign exchange: "They are very cunning, and God knows how, they are able to smell your dollars before you even open your wallet. Then they try to fool you in the way they fool all other tourists. But I used to tell them" - this, in broken Hindi - "go, go, what you thinking, I someone new in

Mumbai? I living here thirty years, yes, thirty, before going phoren' and then they would return to sensible bargaining."

Others told of the way they had made a shrewd deal with shop-keepers who did not know the true value of brass and copper artifacts and knickknacks. These collectors of bric-a-brac, self-appointed connoisseurs of art and antiques, must have acquired their fancies along with their immigration visas. But their number was small, and they never quite succeeded in holding the gathering transfixed in the way that the airline clique managed to. Art was not as popular as airlines were at these evenings.

Six months after Jamshed's trip to Bombay, I received a letter from my brother Percy. Among other things, he wrote about his commitment in the small village:

> Our work with the farmers started very well. They got interest-free loans in the form of seed and fertilizer, which we purchased wholesale, and for the first time in years they did not have to borrow from those blood-thirsty moneylenders.
>
> Ever since we got there, the moneylenders hated us. They tried to persuade us to leave, saying that what we were doing was wrong because we were upsetting the delicate balance of village life and destroying tradition. We, in turn, pointed out things like exploitation, usury, inhumanity, and other abominations whose time was now up. We may have sounded like bold knights-errant, but they turned to threats and said it would soon become so unhealthy for us in the village that we would have to leave quickly enough.
>
> One day when we were out visiting a loan applicant, a farmer who lived close to us brought news that a gang of thugs wielding sticks and cudgels was waiting at the hut - our office and residence. So we stayed the night with the loan applicant and, in the morning, escorted by a band of villagers who insisted on coming along, started for our hut. But there was no hut to return to; it had been razed to the ground during the night, and no one had dared interfere.
>
> Now we are back in Bombay, working on a plan for our return. We have spoken to several news reporters, and our work is getting a lot of publicity. We are also collecting

> fresh donations so that when we go back we will not fail for lack of funds.

Having read this far, I put the letter down for a moment. There you were, my brother, waging battle against corruption and evil, while I was watching sitcoms on my rented Granada TV and attending dinner parties at Parsi homes to listen to chitchat about airlines and airfares.

The rest of the letter concerned Jamshed's visit to Bombay six months ago:

> I wish he'd stayed away, if not from Bombay then at least from me. At best, the time I spent with him was a waste, and while I expected that we would look at things differently, I was not prepared for the crassly materialistic boor that he has turned into. To think he was my "best friend" in school. I have no doubt he believes that the highlight of his visit came when he took some of us to dinner at the Rendezvous - nothing but the most expensive, of course. It was a spectacle to surpass anything he'd done so far. He reminded us from time to time to eat and drink as much as we wanted, without minding the prices, to enjoy ourselves as much as we could, because we wouldn't get a chance to eat here again, at least not till his next visit.
>
> When the soup came, he scolded the waiter that it was cold and sent it back, while the rest of us sat silent and embarrassed. He looked at us nonchalantly, explaining that this was the only way to handle such incompetence; Indians were too meek and docile and should learn to stand up for their rights the way people do in the States.
>
> We were supposed to be impressed by his performance, for we were in an expensive restaurant where only foreign tourists eat on the strength of their U.S. dollars. And here was one of our own, not intimidated within the walls of the five-star Taj Mahal Hotel. In our school days we could only stand outside it and watch the foreigners come and go, wondering what secrets lay inside, what heavenly comforts these fair-skinned superior beings enjoyed. Here was one of our own showing us how to handle it all without feeling a trace of inferiority.
>
> We spent the evening watching Jamshed in disbelief, in silence, which he probably thought was due to the awesome splendour and strangeness of our surroundings.

I was determined not to see him again, not even when he came to say goodbye on the day of his departure, and I don't intend to meet him when he visits Bombay the next time...

As I finished reading, I felt that my brother had been as irritated by Jamshed's presence as I had been by Jamshed's letter six months ago. But I did not write this to Percy; after all, I was planning to be in Bombay in four or five months, and we could talk then. In four more months, I would complete two years in Canada - long enough a separation, I supposed with a naive pomposity, to develop a lucidity of thought which I could carry back with me and bring to bear on all the problems of India.

When the time came, I packed my suitcases with an assortment of gifts: chocolates and cheeses, jams and jellies, pudding and cake mixes, panty hose and stainless steel razor blades - all the items I had seen displayed in the stalls of the "smugglers" along Flora Fountain and which had always been priced out of our reach. I felt like one of those soldiers, who, in times of war, accumulate strange things to use as currency for barter.

Then, arms still sore from the typhoid and cholera inoculations, luggage bursting at the seams with a portable grocery store, and mind suffused with groundless optimism, I boarded the plane.

The aircraft was losing height in preparation for landing. The hard afternoon sun revealed the city I was coming back to after two years. When the plane had taken off two years ago, it had been in the dark of night, and all I saw from the air through shaded, infected eyes were the airport lights of Santa Cruz. But now it was daylight, and I was not wearing dark glasses. I could see the parched land: brown, weary, and unhappy.

A few hours earlier, the aircraft had made its scheduled landing in London, and the aerial landscape had been lush, everywhere, green and hopeful. It enraged me as I contrasted it with what I was now seeing. Gone was the clearness with which I'd promised myself I would look at things. A childish and helpless reaction was all I had left. "It's not fair!" I wanted to stamp my foot and shout, "It's just not fair!"

The first few days in teeming, overpopulated Bombay were difficult. Hostility and tension seemed to be perpetually present in buses, shops, trains. It was disconcerting to discover I'd become unused to this kind of air. Now I knew what soldiers must experience in the trenched after a respite far behind the lines.

I watched almost sick to my stomach when a crowd, clawing its way into a local train, trampled a plastic lunch bag dropped amidst the stampede. When the train departed, the owner sadly yet matter-of-factly picked up the mangle lunch, dusted off one of the chapatis which had slipped out of the bag and waited for the next train. His resignation quickly reminded me that my own reaction was out of proportion to this reality.

After witnessing this incident, I felt I could fit right into it all again. The first flush of confidence appeared in the form of a temptation to run after a bus I'd missed, to leap and join the crowd already hanging out the door. In the old days I would have been off and running without a second thought. I used to pride my agility at this manoeuvre. After all, during rush hour it was the only way to catch a bus, or you'd be left standing at the bus stop with the old and the feeble. It was just one more trick acquired to keep ahead in the daily struggle for survival.

But the bus had moved well into the flow of traffic, and my momentary hesitation gave the game away. It showed me conclusively that my place was with the old and feeble as long as I was here as a tourist and not committed to life in the combat zone.

My brother Percy wrote from the small village that he had been looking forward to meeting me, but: "I cannot come to Bombay right now because I've just heard from Jamshed. He's flying in from New York and writing of things like reunions and great times for all the old crowd. But this is out of the question; I'm not going to see him again."

I wrote back saying I understood.

Our parents were disappointed. They had been looking forward to the family being together for a while. They could not understand why Percy did not like Jamshed anymore, and I'm sure at the back of their minds they thought their son was jealous of his friend because of the fine success he'd made of himself in America. If only they knew the truth; but how was I to explain things to them, and would they understand even if I tried? They truly believed that Jamshed was the smart young fellow, and their son the foolish idealist who forgot that charity begins at home. I felt this trip was not turning out to be anything like I'd hoped it would be: Jamshed was coming and Percy was not, our parents were disappointed with Percy, I was disappointed with them, and in a week I would be flying out of Bombay, confused and miserable.

I left the house without any destination in mind and took the first empty bus that came along. It went to Flora Fountain. The offices were now closing for the day, and crowds would soon spill out of the dirty, yellow-grey buildings, flooding toward bus stops and train stations.

Roadside stalls were open for business, and had been all day, but this would be their busy hour. They were lined up along the edge of the pavement, carefully displaying their merchandise. Here a profusion of towels and napkins from shocking pink to peacock green; there the clatter of pots and pans, all shapes and sizes; further down, a refreshment stall selling sizzling samosas and ice-cold sherbet.

The pavement across the road was the domain of the "smugglers" with their stalls of foreign goods, but they did not interest me, and I stayed on this side of the street. One man was peddling an assortments of toys, calling out as he demonstrated them in turn, "Baba play and baby play! Daddy play and mummy play!" Another, with fiendish vigour, was throwing glass bowls to the ground, yelling "Un-ber-rakable! Un-ber-rakable!"

Sunlight was beginning to fade as I listened to the hawkers singing their tunes to advertise their wares. Kerosene lamps were lit in some of the stalls, punctuating at random the rows on both sides of the road.

Serenely I stood and watched, feeling that there was no real reason for the disappointment which had overcome me earlier that day. All was fine and warm within this moment after sunset, when the lanterns were lit. Perhaps being a visitor had something to do with it, but I was beginning to enjoy myself and starting to feel a part of the crowds which were now flowing down Flora Fountain.

I walked on, when a hand on my shoulder made me turn around. "Bet you weren't expecting to see me in Bombay," said Jamshed.

"As a matter of fact I was," said I. "Percy wrote you were coming." Then I wished I hadn't volunteered this bit of information.

But there was no need to worry about awkward questions regarding Percy. For Jamshed, in fine fettle, had other thoughts he was anxious to share with me.

"So what are you doing here? Some shopping?' he jokingly asked, indicating the little stalls with a disdainful sweep of his hand. "Isn't it terrible the way these buggers think they own the streets - they don't even leave you enough room to walk. The police should drive them off and break up their stalls, really."

He paused, and I wondered if I should say that these people were only trying to earn a meagre living, exercising, amidst a paucity of options, this one; that at least they were not begging or stealing.

But I didn't have a chance. "God, what a racket! It's impossible to take even a quiet little walk in this place. I'll be happy when it's time to catch my plane to New York."

It was hopeless. Jamshed's tone was beginning to resemble that of the letter he'd written the year before from New York. He had then temporarily disturbed the order I was trying to bring into my new life in Toronto, and I'd struck back with a letter of my own. But this time I just wanted to get away from him as quickly as possible. It was as though he was making the peace of mind I was reaching out for dissipate and become forever unattainable.

Suddenly, I understood why Percy did not want to meet him again - he, too, sensed and feared Jamshed's soul-sapping presence.

Around us, all the pavement stalls were immersed in a rich dusk, and each one was now lit by a flickering kerosene lantern. What could I say to Jamshed? What would it take, I wondered, to light the lantern in his soul?

I realized he was waiting for me to speak, so I asked him, perfunctorily, how much longer he would be in Bombay.

"Another week. Seven whole days, and they'll go really slowly. But I'll be dropping in at your place in a couple of days. Let Percy know." We walked together to my bus stop and said goodnight.

On the bus, I thought about what to say if he asked me, two days later, why I hadn't mentioned that Percy was not coming to Bombay.

As it turned out, I did not have to say anything.

Late next evening, Percy was home. I rushed to greet him, but his face showed that he was not returning in this manner as part of a pleasantly planned surprise. Something was dreadfully wrong. His colour was ashen, he was frightened and shaken and struggled to retain his composure.

He tried to smile, as he shook my hand limply, but could not muster the effort to return my hug.

"What's the matter?" said mother. "You don't look well."

Silently, Percy sat down and began to remove his shoes and socks. After a while, he looked up and said, quietly, "They killed Navjeet."

Navjeet was one of their group working with the farmers in the small village.

No one said anything for the next few minutes. Percy sat with his socks dangling from his hands, looking sad, tired, defeated.

Mother rose and said she would make tea. Over tea, Percy told us more about what had happened. Slowly, reluctantly at first, then faster, in a rush, to get the remembering and the telling over with as quickly as possible. "When we returned to the village, the money-lenders were there to make trouble for us. We didn't think they would do anything as serious as the last time because the press was now following our progress and had reported the arson in many newspapers. Yesterday, we were out at the wholesaler's. We were ordering seed for next year, but Navjeet had stayed behind to work on the accounts. When we returned, he was lying unconscious on the floor...his face and head were bleeding badly...we carried him to the makeshift clinic in the village - there is no hospital...the doctor said there was severe internal damage...massive head injuries...a few hours later he was dead."

Percy stayed home all next day, even though he knew Jamshed was coming to visit. The brutality had sickened him and he did not feel like doing anything or going anywhere. This was not normal for my brother, but then, neither was the experience he'd been through. Something was needed to help him get over it. And, strangely enough, it was Jamshed who unwittingly provided this something.

When he arrived in the evening, mother asked him how he'd been enjoying his trip so far. He replied, true to form, "Oh auntie, I'm tired of this place, really. The dust and the heat and the crowds - I've had enough of it." And mother nodded sympathetically.

Soon, the moment Percy had been dreading was at hand. Mother asked him to narrate, for Jamshed's benefit, the events which had brought him home so suddenly. But Percy just shook his head, so she told the story herself.

When she'd finished, Jamshed could not contain himself. "I told you from the beginning that all this was a waste of time and nothing would come of it, remember? I hope you don't mind my saying this, but I still think the best thing for you to do is to come to the States, there is so much you could achieve over there. There, if you are good, you are appreciated, and you get ahead. Not like here, where everything is controlled by uncles and aunts..."

I watched my brother, certain that he would finally allow his exasperation with Jamshed to spill and say all the things that were surely choking him.

But when Jamshed concluded his harangue, Percy calmly turned to mother and said quietly, "Could we have dinner right away? I'm going to arrange a meeting with my friends at eight o'clock. We must decide on our next move in the village."

Five days later, I was back in Toronto. Gradually, I discovered I'd brought back with me my entire burden of riddles and puzzles, unsolved. The whole sorry package was there, not lightened at all. The epiphany would have to wait for another time, another trip.

I mused, I gave way to whimsy: I Tiresias, throbbing between two lives, humbled by the ambiguities and dichotomies confronting me...

I thought of Jamshed and his refusal to enjoy his trips to India, his way of seeing the worst in everything. Was he too waiting for some epiphany and growing impatient because it kept him from accepting life in America? Perhaps the contempt and disdain which he shed were only his way of lightening his own load.

That Christmas I received a card from Jamshed. The Christmas seal, postage stamp, and address label were all neatly and correctly in place, like everything else about his surface existence. But I put down the envelope without opening it, wondering if this innocuous outer shell concealed more of his confusion, disdain, arrogance.

Then, my mind made up, I walked out of the apartment, down the hallway, and dropped the envelope through the chute of the garbage incinerator.

10

The Cage

by
Neil Bissoondath

Born in Trinidad in 1955, Neil is one of the exciting younger talents to join the Canadian literary mosaic. Emigrating to Canada in 1973, he attended York University. Having taught English and French for some time, he now writes full time.

My father is an architect. Architects are good at designing things: stores, houses, apartments, prisons. For my mother, my father, not an unkind man, designed a house. For me, my father, not a kind man, designed a cage.

My father is a proud man. He traces his ancestry back nine generations. Our family name is well known in Yokohama, not only because of my father's architectural firm but also because of those nine generations: his name is my father's greatest treasure.

It is not mine.

At the Shinto shrine in the backyard my father mumbles the names of his ancestors, calling on them, invoking their presence. With those names he swears, expresses pleasure, offers compliments. He knows those names better than he knows mine.

When I was small, I used to stand at the window of the living room watching my father as he mumbled before the shrine. He almost always wore a grey turtleneck sweater; he suffered from asthma and said that the air that blew in off the sea, over the American warships and docks, came heavy with moisture and oil. On especially damp mornings he would return to the house with the skin under his eyes greyed and his cheeks scarlet. He coughed a great deal, and I could see his chest labouring rhythmically beneath his sweater.

I often wondered why, even on the worst of mornings, with drizzle and grey mist, he went out to the shrine: couldn't the ancestors wait a day? A few hours? Were they so demanding? One day I asked him why and he just stared back at me in silence. He never answered. Maybe be couldn't. Maybe it was just something he knew deep within him, an urge he bowed to without understanding. Maybe it was to him, as to me, a mystery.

I shall never forget the day he called me Michi, the name of his father's mother. She was the person he loved best in the world, and for many years after her death he would visit her grave, to cry. He called me Michi because he had simply forgotten my name. He became angry when my mother reminded him.

When I was a child he took only occasional notice of me. I was my mother's charge. He was not a bad father. He was just as much of one as he was capable of being. His concerns were less immediate.

His attention grew during the teenage years, for he feared them most. When I was fifteen, I told my parents I no longer wanted to take piano lessons. I saw distress on my mother's face: she had, in her youth, before marriage, wanted to be a concert pianist. When I practised, she would often sit quietly behind me, listening, saying nothing. I could feel her ears reaching out to every key my fingers hit, every sound my touch produced. At times I felt I was playing not for me but for her, giving her through the pain and fatigue in my fingers a skein of memory. But music cannot be a duty. It must come naturally. I am not a musician. I grew bored. My fingers on the piano keys produced a lifeless sound. My father, admitting this, agreed to let me stop. My father, after quietly invoking his ancestors, said it was a bad sign. But he would agree if I accepted the *Ko-to* in place of the piano.

I agreed. It gave me my way and allowed him to assert his authority.

However, his distrust of my age continued. One day he searched among my clothes and found a packet of letters. It was a modest collection, three from girlfriends in foreign places, one from a boy I had known briefly in school. His family had moved to Osaka and he had written me this one letter, a friendly letter, a letter to say hello. My father ignored the letters from my girlfriends and handed me the letter from the boy. He demanded that I read it to him: a friendly letter, a silly letter; finally, a humiliating letter. When I finished, he took the letter with him. I never saw it again. At dinner that evening he searched my eyes for signs of crying. He saw none. He exchanged worried glances with my mother.

I hadn't cried. Instead, I had thought; and the lesson I learned was far greater than mere distrust of my father. I learnt, more than anything else, how little of my life was my own, in my father's eyes. It was the horror of this that prevented tears; his claim to my privacy that, finally, caused me to regard him with eyes of ice.

I had few friends. My peers and I had little in common. They liked to talk of husbands, babies, houses; boredom was my response. No simple explanation offered itself, nor did I seek one. Maybe it was my age, maybe it was my temperament, but I accepted this situation. Often, in the middle of a gathering of schoolmates, I would slip away home, to my room.

For there, among my school texts, was my favorite companion, a child's book that had been a gift many years before from my father. It was a large book, with hard covers and pages of a thick, velvety paper. It related the story of the first foreigners to come to Japan. Every other page contained an illustration, of the sea, of the ships, of the mountains of Japan, in colors so bright they appeared edible.

The picture that most attracted me presented the first meeting between foreigners and Samurai. They stood, clusters of men, facing one another: foreigners to the right, grotesquely bearded, drab in seafaring leathers; Samurai to the left, resplendent in outfits of patterned and folded color. Behind them, with a purity borne only in the imagination, lay a calm, blue sea tinged here and there by whitecaps of intricate lace. On the horizon, like a dark brown stain on the swept cleanliness of the sky, sat the foreigners' ship.

My father, in giving me the book, had stressed the obvious: the ugliness of the foreigners, the beauty of the Samurai. But my mind was gripped by the roughness, the apparent unpredictability, of the foreigners. The Samurai were of a cold beauty; you knew what to expect of them, and in this my father saw virtue. For me, the foreigners were creatures who could have exploded with a suddenness that was like charm. Looking at them, I wondered about their houses, their food, their families. I wanted to know what they thought and how they felt. This to me was the intrigue of the book, and I would spend many hours struggling with the blank my mind offered when I tried to go beyond the page before me.

I remember one day asking my father to tell me about the foreigners. He was immediately troubled. He said, "They came from Europe." But what did the word "Europe" mean, I asked. Europe: to me, a word without flesh. "This is an unnecessary question," he replied, his eyes regarding the book and me with suspicion. I took the book from his hands and returned to my room.

Not long after this I showed the book to a school friend. We were both about twelve years old at the time and I hoped to find companionship of spirit. She looked through the book and handed it back to me, saying nothing. I asked her opinion of it. She said, "It is a very pretty book." And those words, so simple, so empty, created distance between us.

The book has remained in my room ever since, safe, undisplayed.

At eighteen, when I graduated from high school, my parents tried to marry me off. He was an older man from my father's firm, an architect like my father. They made me wear a kimono to meet him. At first his glances were modest, but as the evening wore on he became bolder. Angered, I returned his searching gazes. He faltered. He became modest once again. Finally, he left.

My behavior had not gone unnoticed. Afterwards my mother scolded me.

I said, "I do not want to marry."

My mother said, "The choice is not yours, it is not any woman's."

My father said nothing. He left the room.

My mother said, "You have made your father very angry."

I said, "I do not want to marry. I want to live with a man."

My mother looked at me as if I had gone mad. "We are sending you to university. You will not waste your education in such a way."

"I want to have a career."

"We are not giving you an education so you can work. Men want educated wives."

"I do not want to be a man's wife."

"Where are you getting such ideas? You associate with the wrong people. Such ideas are foreign to us." Then she too left the room.

The "wrong people" has always been one of my mother's obsessions. I remember inviting a schoolmate to my house. She met my mother. They talked. When my friend left, my mother said, "I do not think you should associate with such people." I was still obedient at the time; I never spoke to the girl again. I understood why my mother took this attitude. The girl's home was in one of the poorer sections of Yokohama, her mother worked as a clerk in a department store. This was the first time my mother was too busy to drive one of my friends home. And for me, guilt came only years later, too late, as with everything in retrospect.

My mother. She once played the piano. She has a degree in opera from Tokyo University. She could have had a career. Instead, she got married. She talks of her life now only to say she is happy. But what is this happiness--who can say? Not I, for I could never be happy in her situation. I maybe know too much. Yet I cannot contradict my mother. I can only say I doubt her. This self-sacrifice--she has given her all to her husband, to her son, to me; she has rejected all possibility of leading her own life, of developing her talent--this self-sacrifice is not for me. She has the ability to put up with things even when she is at odds with them. I suppose this shows strength. Sometimes, though, I wonder if this is not so much strength as a simple lack of choice. My mother does not have the ability to create choice where there is none.

I am, in the end, tangible proof of my mother's failure as a woman.

Once during this same summer that ushered me from high school to university my mother expressed a desire to spend the vacation in Kyoto. My father said he wished to visit Kobe; he was adamant. Later, I heard my father, unaware of my presence, telling my brother to observe his handling of the situation. All along, he said, he had wanted to visit Kyoto but be would let my mother beg a little, cajole him, fawn over him; only then would he agree to visit Kyoto. My mother would think she had won a great victory. And that was the way it worked out. My mother never realized the deception, and sadness prevented me from revealing it to her. It was too, I knew, part of the game she had long ago accepted.

My mother and women like her, my father and men like him, will tell you that the man's world is in his office, the woman's in her house. But in my parents' house, designed by my father, built by him, his word is law. My mother, if she really believes in the division of domain, lives in a world of illusion.

This facility for seeing the wrong thing, asking the wrong question, already a barrier between acquaintanceship and friendship, made my relations with my brother difficult. I resented having chores to do--washing dishes, making beds, both his and mine, cleaning the house--while his only duty was to protect the family name by staying out of trouble. I resented having my telephone callers interrogated, my letters scanned, my visitors judged, while he was free to socialize with people of his own choosing. I resented the late hours he was permitted to keep while I was forced to spend my evening practising the *Ko-to*, producing music that bored me to tears and put my father in mind of his ancestors, never far out of reach. I resented my brother's freedom to choose from among the girls he knew while I could meet only those men selected by my father, always architects, always older, always pained by courtship conducted before the boss.

My brother and I have never spoken. He is as much a stranger to me as I am to him. What I know of him I do not like. He is too much like my father. They occasionally pray together at the shrine in the backyard.

I had been accepted at Tokyo University, in dietetics. This field was not my choice, but my father's. From a magazine article he had got the idea that dietetics would be a fine, harmless profession, and one easily dropped for marriage. I would have preferred literature but I had no choice. It was my father's money that afforded me an education, and his connections that brought me entry to prestigious Tokyo University.

I left for Tokyo at the end of the summer, with my mother as temporary chaperone. She settled me in and, after three days, left with the lightest of kisses. She had grown into her role, my mother, and had spent much of her time with me worrying about my father and brother. The moment she left, uncertainty became my sole companion. I was as tentative as a spider's web in wind. I avoided people, grew close to no one. My life was my books, and I emerged from chemistry and anatomy only to attend the occasional gathering organized by the dietetics department. Attendance at these "social evenings" was informally obligatory: even in the wider world, you belonged to a family and owed certain obligations. Nothing exciting ever happened at these parties. You went, you drank a little, ate a little, chatted politely, you left. Little was achieved, save homage to the concept of the group. Maybe occasionally a student would get a low grade raised a little.

It was at one of these gatherings halfway through my first year at university that I met Keisuke, a well-know Japanese poet. I had never heard of him, for my father, probably remembering the childhood incident with my story book, had proscribed literature. So at first I treated Keisuke in an off-hand manner. I distrusted his name, Keisuke, a fine old traditional name; it seemed to reflect all the values my father held dear. Nor was he particularly attractive in any way. His physique was undistinguished, tending, if anything, to softness around the middle; and the whites of his eyes were scrawled by a complicated system of red veins, from lack of sleep. At one point in the evening, I heard him say that it was his habit to drop in when he could on the gatherings of the different departments. This declaration, made not to me but to a group that had politely formed around him, scared me a little. It was not something that was done and, although there was a general assent that this was a good idea, I could see the hesitation that preceded the required politeness, the easy discomfort quickly submerged in nods and smiles. And I could see, too, that Keisuke had not missed it. He looked at me and smiled: we shared a secret.

After, when he had left, there were a few whispered comments about how odd he was. One of the professors, a small, balding man, said slyly, "But he's a poet. You know what *they're* like..."

The next day at lunch in the cafeteria, Keisuke appeared at my table and sat down, without asking permission. "So," he said. "Did they find me very odd?"

Flustered at hearing the same word in his mouth as had been used to describe him the previous evening, I instinctively said, "Yes."

For a second there was silence, and then we both began laughing. Our secret, understood by a smile the evening before, was made explicit by the laughter. I became comfortable with him. He asked me to call him "Kay", and he mocked his own name, describing it with the English word "stuffy", which he had to explain to me since my English was not very good at the time.

We talked a great deal. He told me he had lived and studied in America for seven years. His father, an executive with the Panasonic Corporation, had been transferred to New Jersey when Kay was sixteen. Kay knew New York City well, and as he described it--the lights, the noise, the excitement--I wondered why he had returned, after all that time, to Japan.

He smiled at my question. "I am Japanese," he said.

I nodded, but the answer discomforted me. It was my father's explanation of too many things.

Kay and I became friends. He invited me to his apartment not far from the university. It was a small place, and cluttered. On the walls he had hung framed American film posters, all at different heights so that any thought of uniformity was banished. Everywhere--on his desk, on the coffee table, on the kitchen counters-he had stacked books and magazines and papers. We would sit together in a corner on a *tatami*, reading or talking under the yellow light of a wall-lamp.

I told him about my father, my mother, my brother. He showed me some of his poetry. I read it. I understood little. He asked what literature I had read. I told him about my father's prohibition on books and of his final admonition on the night before I left for Tokyo. Stay away, he had said, from books full of fine words. Kawabata, Tanizaki, Mishima would not help my chemistry marks and, besides, writers always had strange ideas anyway, ideas unfit for young female minds.

Kay listened to my story in silence. Then he said, "Your father is a man full of fears." This was like revelation to me.

I confessed that I had read Mishima, for my brother had on the bookshelves in his room the complete works, a gift from our father. I had read them surreptitiously and, at the time, untrained, unaware, I had seized only upon the eroticism. Kay, unsurprised, explained to me what I had missed: the mingling of the sex with blood, and the brooding sense of violence. "Mishima was mad in many respects," he said. "A twentieth-century

Samurai. His end was fitting." And now, now that I understand Mishima, I worry about my brother, and I fear him.

One evening, after a light dinner of *sashimi* and warm sake, Kay seduced me. As I write this, I realize what an un-Japanese admission it is. It scares me a little.

After, lying on the *tatami*, smoking my first cigarette and enjoying the warmth and soreness that clasped my body, I felt as if I had been given a precious key, but a key to what I wasn't sure. This too Kay, lying wet next to me, understood. He suggested I read Ibsen and, in the following months as my first year of university drew to a close, he supplied translations to help my shaky English through the Ibsen texts he'd studied in America. We discussed his works, among others, and the more intense our discussions became, the more I found myself articulating thoughts and ideas that would have made my father blue with rage.

Kay, one of those writers with strange ideas whom my father so feared, gave me the ability to put into words what had been for me, until then, ungrasped feelings. With his help, I arrived at last at a kind of self-comprehension, although a confusion--guilt, Kay call it--remained. He said this was so because, although my ideas were coming into focus, their source remained hidden.

However, I do not want to give the impression that I always sailed smoothly. At times, especially after another of the tedious meetings with one of my father's architects--for which I was periodically called home--I felt that the seduction was less a key than a betrayal. As I sat there in my father's spare living room, serving the men, smiling at them, I felt that Kay had heightened my confusion rather than diminished it. But these periods of doubt were shortlived.

The rest of my university career was uneventful. Kay and I continue to see one another from time to time but the intimacy of that first year was never repeated. He had too much work, I had too much work. At least, it was the excuse we used.

I graduated as a dietician and had no trouble finding a job in a hospital in Yokohama. I worked there for a year, in a profession not of my choosing, counting day after day the calorie intake of patients. Counting calories becomes tedious after a while and the patients soon became little more than mathematical sums in my mind, defining themselves by what they could eat.

At the end of one particularly trying day, I called on a patient, an old woman, chronically ill and querulous, to discuss her rejection of prescribed food. She explained to me in a cross voice that she wanted, of all things, mayonnaise on her food. I told her this was impossible. She became abusive. I became abusive. I hit her with my clipboard. She started to cry, silently, like a child, the tears filling the wrinkles and creases of her crumpled face. It was then, looking at her through my own tears, that I realized I could not continue.

The tedium of the job, living once more in my father's house, smiling at his architects, practising the *ko-to*, these were all taking their toll on me.

I confronted my parents with my decision. They offered an alternative. They had never been happy about my working; a working wife is in short demand. It would be better, they said, if I were to concentrate on what really mattered. I was getting old, already twenty-three. In five or six years I would be considered an old maid, an also-ran in the race to the conjugal bed. I had better get cracking.

But, as usual, I had my own idea. I had managed to save a tidy sum during my year of work, money my father considered part of a future marriage contract. In Japan, women marry not for love but for security. The man acquires a kind of maid-for-life. For a person with ideas, marriage means compromise, an affair not of the heart but of the bank account. Therefore, my savings compensated a bit for my advanced age and my father never failed to mention the money when one of the suitors called.

I, however, wanted to travel. My father said it was out of the question; neither he nor my mother could leave Yokohama at the time. I said I wanted to travel alone. My father said this was preposterous, and he called on his ancestors, all nine generations of them, to witness the madness of his daughter.

Kay had once said to me, "Learn from the past but never let it control you." I think it was a line from one of his poems. At that moment the line ran through my mind. If my past would not control me, I decided, then neither would my father's. I told them I was leaving. My father threatened to restrain me physically. He called my brother to help. He came. I did not protest; it would have served no purpose. My father and brother were as one. Even their eyes, black circles trapped behind the same thick lenses, framed by the same black plastic, were indistinguishable. It was these eyes that I saw come at me. As they led me off between them, my mother started crying. But she said nothing. They locked me in my room and told the hospital I was sick.

For a week I lay or sat alone in my room. My mother, silent always, brought me my meals, of which I ate little. I slept a lot, tried to read, spent long hours looking at my picture book: the splendid Samurai, the bearded foreigners. At one point--I no longer remember whether it was day or night; time, after a while, was of no importance--I felt myself slipping into the painting, becoming part of it. I could feel the weight of heavy sea air on my face, the soft tingle of sand beneath my feet; I could hear the broken whisper of softly tumbling surf. I was prepared to surrender myself but something--a voice, a rattle of dishes--tugged me back. For the first time in my captivity, I cried. My tears fell onto the pages of my book and there the stains remain.

They let me out after a week and I returned to work. My father had spoken to the administrator of the hospital, an old friend. Since other members of the staff had complained about the old woman's behavior, no action was taken against me, save a kindly lecture on the virtues of patience.

The next two months were, however, not easy. I was never allowed a moment to myself; my every movement was monitored, every minute accounted for. Even at work, I found out, the administrator asked discreet questions about me. My father had spoken to him about more than my problems with the old woman.

My life became like that of the four song-birds my brother kept in bamboo cages suspended from the ceiling of his room. They would whistle and chirp every morning, each making its own distinct cry, sometimes sounding as if in competition against one another. The birds would sing at precisely the same time every morning, demanding food. I thought they saw this ability to wake him as power, but my brother knew who controlled the food.

One day, with the sense of reserved delight he shared with our father, my brother brought home a new song-bird. It was the smallest of them all, a tiny creature of a blue and red that sparkled when brushed by the sun. But there was a problem: while the others sang, this new bird remained silent. My brother tried coaxing music out of him, in vain. He tried attacking with a stick, but the bird was unmoved. My brother first tried withholding food, but later when the incentive was offered the bird ignored it, and twice he knocked over his dish, scattering the seed.

The bird uttered only one sound in his week in my brother's bedroom, a pure, shrill whistle. The cry brought my brother, my mother, and me to the room. The bird was lying on the floor of the cage. My brother opened the door and poked the little body with finger, at first gently, then more roughly. Satisfied it was dead, he picked it up by a wing, took it to the kitchen, and dropped it into the garbage can. He dusted his hands casually and returned to his breakfast. He showed no regret.

I watched my brother with horror. At that moment I hated him. I went to my room and I cried, for the bird, for myself.

He replaced it that evening with a more pliant bird. This one sang easily, and it was fed.

The next day I began playing the traditional daughter. I quit my job, I never complained, I welcomed the architects, smiled at them, hinted to my father of grandchildren: a game, a game for which my real personality had to be hidden away like the pregnant, unwed daughter of a rich family. It was not very difficult, for I discovered in myself a strange determination.

After two months of this, my father, watchful always, put his suspicions aside. He said to my mother, "I have exercised the power of my ancestors. They cannot be resisted." Then he went to visit the grave of Michi, his father's mother.

During this period I grew closer to my mother, for she was most often my guard. One night--it turned out to be my last in my father's house--we sat talking in my room. We had turned off the lights and opened the window. Above the silhouetted trees and roof tops, we could see the sky turning dark, as if expiring. As yet, no stars were visible. The night air was cool and we could hear insects chirping and cluttering in the shrubbery outside. My mother put on a sweater over her kimono, an oddly touching sight, and folded her arms, not sternly as I had once thought, but wearily, like a woman undone. We sat on the bed, I on one side, she on the other, with a great expanse between us.

I asked her, "Have you ever thought of the possibility of leading your own life?"

She sighed. "I used to think of it when I was small but I always knew it would be impossible."

"Why?"

"You are playing games now." She smiled sadly. Without looking at me, she said, "Whatever happens, I am always your mother. Wherever you are, whatever you are doing, you can call me. I will help."

"Who can you call?"

"Your father."

"You once had friends."

"Yes, but your father comes first. Friends just ..." She waved her hands, searching for words. "...just get in the way."

"But you haven't got any friends."

"I am content. I have all I want, all I need. Now say no more about it."

I couldn't see her face. She was all in shadow. But her voice was tender.

The next day, for the first time in many months, she left me alone, unguarded. I packed my bags and called a taxi. The night before, although I hadn't known it, she had been telling me goodbye.

I had always believed I could trust none of my relatives: my father, made in the image of his ancestors; my mother, made in the image of my father; my brother, a stranger. It took me a long time to realize that my mother was my friend. I do not think she really understood me but I was one of those things she put up with even though we were at odds. I hope she can one day understand my attitude but I do not expect this. I can only hope.

I spent two months in Tokyo, in an apartment lent to me by one of Kay's friends. Kay visited me from time to time. We couldn't talk. He seemed uncomfortable with me and, through this, I became uncomfortable with him. We were like polite strangers. This distance, and the silences it brought with it, depressed me; and I, in turn, depressed him.

One evening, after a particularly silent dinner, I asked him to tell me exactly what was wrong.

He said, "Nothing." Then he closed his eyes and said, "I have not been able to write. Your mood effects me. It is not good."

I couldn't reply. There was nothing to say.

He opened his eyes, the whites red-veined, the skin around them reddened, and looked slowly around the apartment. It was very much like his, the film posters, the stacks of books and magazines. He had started a style among his friends.

"There is something else, too," he finally said. "I have been wondering...well, do you think you did the correct thing in leaving your father's house?'

I looked at him: it was all I could do. The one person of whom I had been sure. I said, "Keisuke. Keisuke."

He left a few minutes later, after putting the dishes into the kitchen sink.

His visits grew less frequent and finally stopped altogether. Without him, I found myself enmeshed in the freedom I had sought, friendless, guideless, at liberty to choose my own way. "Without him": the irony does not escape me.

I found a job, again ironically, playing the piano in a bar. I eventually moved into my own little apartment and developed a small circle of friends, all connected in one way or the other with the bar. One night the owner, an overweight man who dressed in flashy American clothes, tried to pressure me into sleeping with him. I never went back to the bar and so had yet another place to avoid, another place to run from.

In Tokyo, anonymity was easy to obtain: it is not difficult to be alone in a crowd of thousands. Privacy came more easily in large, overpopulated Tokyo than in the smaller, relatively slow-paced Yokohama. Tokyo, the least traditional, most western, of our cities is, for me, the safest.

But it was still Japan. I was invited to parties. Japanese parties, like marriages, are business occasions in disguise. Men go to a party to get a promotion or to clinch a deal. The women smile and serve. The men drink and talk. When they have drunk enough, they talk sex and arrange package tours to Korea, where they enjoy the prostitutes of a people they detest.

I felt I had to get away. My first thought was: Europe. But I quickly realized there were yet other places I had to avoid, the usual Japanese destinations: much of Europe, much of America, especially Boston or Philadelphia or New York. So I changed my money to travellers' cheques and bought a plane ticket to Toronto. It was new space. I expected nothing.

Many Japanese think of snow and bears and wonderful nature like Niagara Falls when they think off Canada. But Toronto, a big city, bigger than Tokyo, less crowded, with more trees and flowers, did not surprise me. I do not know if it was Toronto or me. Probably me.

I rented a room in a big house across from a park. My landlady, Mrs. Harris, lived on the first floor with her sister, Mrs. Duncan, and her cat, Ginger. She was a small woman of about fifty, with hair too blonde for her age. "We are all widows," she said with a smile the first time I went to the house. "Ginger's Tom died last week. A car, poor dear." I thought her a strange woman but she smiled often, the skin on her face stretching into congruent wrinkles.

The second floor was rented to people I never saw. But they liked rock music. Their stereo worked every day, from early morning to late at night. I rarely heard the music but I was always aware of it because of the thump of the bass beneath my feet, like a heart beating through the worn green carpet.

The third floor was divided into two small rooms. It was one of these that I took. The ceiling followed the contours of the roof, and the walls were painted a white that reflected the little sunlight that came in through the small window. The furniture was sparse: a bed, an easy chair, a table with a lamp. My window overlooked the top of trees and, to the left, fenced-in tennis courts. Sometimes, on a clear day, I could see Lake Ontario on the horizon, a thin ribbon of blue barely distinguishable from the sky.

I did little in my first weeks in Toronto. I walked. I visited the tourist sights. I learned my way around the city. The last heat of the summer exploded down from the sky every day. It exhausted me, and I spent much time sleeping. My memories of the time are dull, everything seems to have rounded corners, everything seems somehow soft.

On weekends, many people came to the park across the street, to walk, to eat, to talk. I would sit at my window observing them, many forms in blue denim or shades of brown, the occasional red or yellow or purple: glimpses of lives I would never touch, for I stayed at my window.

Looking. Looking. Looking.

One hot afternoon, returning groggy from my walk, I came across my third-floor neighbour sitting in the small front porch. She was a tall lady with red hair and very white skin. Perspiration slicked her forehead. She wore a thin white T-shirt and shorts. In her right hand she held an open beer bottle.

"Hello," she said as I walked up the stairs. "Hot, isn't it."

I said, "Yes," reaching for the doorknob. It was no cooler on the porch than it had been in the sun, only the heat was different. Out there, the sunlight burned like an open flame; here, it was like steam. I was exhausted. I did not want to deplete the last of my energy by talking. English was still a strain.

"It's like a goddam oven up here," she said, pushing a chair towards me. "Hell, it's like a goddam oven down here. But at least it's open."

I sat down. We had seen each other twice before but each time she had been in a hurry. I had been shy. We had just said hello.

"You from Hong Kong?" She asked.

"No, I am from Tokyo. I am Japanese." Across the street, the browned grass of the park cowered in the shadow of the trees.

"Oh." She sipped from her beer. "What are you doing here?"

"I plan to take English lessons." My words surprised me. It had been something to say, an excuse for being there, but as I heard myself I thought it a good idea.

"Oh." Then there was silence. On the road a car sped by in a spasm of loud music.

"What do you do?" I finally asked; it took courage.

"I dance. I'm a dancer. My name is Sherry."

"Ballet?Jazz?"

"Table."

"Tables?"

"I work in a strip joint."

"What is `strip joint', please?"

She laughed. "It's a place where ladies like me take off their clothes. For men."

"*Hai*. Yes. I see." The heavy air wrapped itself around my skin like a steamed napkin, and for a second I smelled the oily brine of the Yokohama harbour. "Excuse me, please," I said getting up. The smell, as brief and as powerful as vision, had frightened me.

She watched me open the door. "Like a goddam oven," she said.

The next day I checked the Yellow Pages for a school and went down to their office. It was on the edge of the Yorkville area, a place of expensive stores and restaurants. The side-walks were crowded: many young people with perfect hair and clothes; many old people trying to look like the young people. On one corner a young man with a clown's face juggled colored balls for a small crowd. On another, a young couple in tuxedos played violins while people hurried by.

I was uncomfortable among these people: their numbers didn't offer anonymity. It was just the opposite, in fact. The people, by their dress, by their extravagance of behavior, demanded to be noticed: they were on display. I walked quickly to the office building where the school was located, into the lobby of marble that created echo in the fall of my footsteps, into the elevator that at last brought relief.

Behind the green door that carried only a number, a man with grey hair and glasses was sitting at a desk. In front of him were a telephone, an ashtray so full that the ashes formed a little mountain, and a messy pile of papers. He was playing Scrabble when I walked in, a rack with tiles at either side of the board. No one else was in the office; he was playing against himself, right hand against left hand.

"Good morning," he said, standing up. "Can I help you?" His suit, of a dark blue, showed chalk smudges at the pockets and on the right shoulder.

"Yes, please, I wish to improve my English language."

He offered me a seat and went to another room to get coffee. The walls of the office were bare; in the far corner a large climbing plant, green leaves dulled by dust, clung weakly to its wooden staff.

He returned with two Styrofoam cups of coffee. He placed one on the desk in front of me, the other on the Scrabble board. As he sat down he asked me if I was from Hong Kong. Then he told me about himself. He spoke some French, some Spanish, some German. He had lived and worked in many places. He didn't like Greek food, cats, and American cigarettes. Finally, after an hour, he told me about the school and we managed to arrange private English lessons for me.

I began the following week. My teacher, a tall, nervous young man with a moustache, was a student at the University of Toronto. He dressed poorly, and was so thin and white that at times, under the fluorescent light of the classroom--desk, chairs, walls bare but for the black rectangle of the chalk board--I thought I could see through him. He said he was a vegetarian.

He wanted to talk about Japan and *hara-kiri*, although he knew nothing about Japan or *hara-kiri*. We discussed food. He insisted that I, being a Japanese person, never ate bread, only rice and vegetables and raw fish and nothing else. He would not believe that I had tasted my first Big Mac in Tokyo.

At one point he said, "Ahh, yes, I understand. American imperialism."

"No," I replied. "Good taste."

He did not appreciate my attempt at humor. He became angry and drilled me severely on grammar and vocabulary, refusing to discuss anything.

I settled in to a routine: Classes every morning at the school; a light lunch, then a walk in the afternoon; back to my hot room for a nap; dinner at a restaurant and then my room again, for homework and reading. It was an easy, uncomplicated life. For the first time I knew what it was to anticipate the next day without tension.

Sometimes I saw Sherry, my third-floor neighbour. We would exchange a few words of politeness. Once she asked my opinion of a perfume she had bought. Another time she held up to herself a new blouse. Through these brief encounters, I grew comfortable with her, even to like her a little.

My one shadow was a nightmare. Gentle and vivid, it came again and again, at first sporadically, later with greater frequency: my father and Keisuke, both in the dress of Samurai, standing on a beach, swords unsheathed, while behind them the sea wept with voice of my mother. I would awake with the sound off sobbing in my ears and I would have to speak to myself: *I am in Toronto. I am in Toronto.*

Toronto: a place where my personality could be free, it was not a city of traditions in a country of traditions. It was America, in the best implication that word held for us Japanese: bright, clean, safe, new. Life experienced without the constraints of an overwhelming past. I shall never forget my joy when, awaking one night in a sweat from the nightmare, I realized that here I was a young person and not almost an old maid, that by a simple plane flight I had found rejuvenation.

For two months I lived with a joy I had never imagined possible, the joy of an escape that did not demand constant confrontation with the past.

At the school, the director's hands continued to challenge one another to Scrabble. My teacher grew thinner, shaved his moustache, grew it back, added a beard. I practised grammar, vocabulary, sentence structure.

I was so comfortable I even wrote a short note to my mother, to let her know I was all right.

Summer began signalling its end. The trees across the street lost some of their green; the heat of the day was less severe and at night my room cooled enough that I needed to cover myself with a sheet. At school, I got a new teacher. The first had come in one morning with the shaved head and salmon robes of a religious cult, and had spent much of one class trying to convince me to drop English in favor of Hindi. He was fired.

One evening I saw Sherry in the restaurant where I had dinner. I was surprised, for she usually worked in the evenings.

"How's your English?" she said loudly, motioning me to her table.

"Fine, thank you. I have learnt much. How are you?" I sat down. She had already eaten. The plate before her was empty but for smeared ketchup.

"Not so great. Can't work."

"I am sorry. Are you sick?"

"Not quite. I had an operation."

"It is not serious, I hope."

She laughed. "No. I had a tit job."

"Pardon me, I do not understand."

"They cut my breast open. Cleaned 'em out. Put in bags of water. Size makes money."

"*Hai.* Yes. I see." Suddenly I was no longer hungry. My eyes swept involuntarily from her face to the table.

She pushed her chair and picked up her cigarettes. "It hurts," she said softly, a look of pain on her face. "I better go." She stood up. Her face turned into the light. I saw bags under her eyes, wrinkles I had not noticed before, and I realized I had never before seen her without makeup. The light shone through her curled hair, thinning it like an old person's. "See you, " she said.

"Yes, sleep well." I watched her go, feeling her take some of my joy with her.

Two weeks later, as I was doing my homework late at night, I was disturbed by noises from Sherry's room. I put my book down and listened. At first there was nothing. Then I heard a quiet groan. I became worried. I went to my door and listened again. Another groan. I opened my door, put my head into the corridor, and said, "Sherry, what is it, please?" I listened. There was no answer, no sound. Uncertain, I closed my door and went back to my books. A few minutes later, Sherry's door slammed and heavy footsteps hurried down the stairs. The front door slammed.

My door flew open. Sherry walked in slowly. She was wearing a bathrobe. "Well, little Miss Jap, you pleased with your work?" She was calm, but it was the calm of anger, the same restraint my father and brother displayed in times of emotion.

"I am sorry?" I put down my book.

"You just cost me two hundred dollars."

"I do not understand."

"'*What is it please, Sherry?*'" she mimicked me. "The john went soft on me. You think I got paid? Eh? That's two hundred dollars I'm out of, lady."

"Who is John, please?"

"Jesus Christ! What are they teaching you at that school, anyways?"

I was very confused. I said, "I am sorry. Please explain."

"What are you? Some kinda moron?" Then she turned and walked backed to her room. Her door slammed.

I got up and closed my door. It was getting cold in the room. I shut the window and got into bed, pulling the sheet tightly up to my neck. That night my nightmare came again: my father, Keisuke, and my mother weeping like the sea.

When I came in from school the next day, Mrs. Harris the landlady called me into the kitchen. She was sitting at the dining table with Mrs. Duncan, Ginger the cat on her lap. The little television next to the fridge was on but the sound was turned down.

Mrs. Harris said, "About last night, my dear, I just wanted to let you know it won't happen again. Sherry's gone. I asked her to leave this morning."

"What happened last night, please? I do not understand." I had tried to seek an explanation from my teacher at the school but, upon hearing the story, she had grown uneasy and talked about the English subjunctive.

"Oh dear," said Mrs. Harris. She glanced at Mrs. Duncan.

"Well, you see, dear, she was a stripper. Do you know what that means?"

"I know. She told me." Mrs. Duncan held out a plate of cookies to me. I took one.

"And sometimes, quite often in fact I found out this morning, she brought men back to her room with her. They paid her, you see. To...well, you know."

"*Hai.* Yes. I see." I understood now, with horror, the two hundred dollars.

"But she's gone now, thank God."

I went up to my room, the cookies growing moist where the tips of my fingers pressed into it. The door to Sherry's room was open, the bed stripped, the dresser and table cleared of cosmetics and perfumes Sherry collected. Beneath my feet, the neighbours' stereo beat in its steady palpitations. I felt very alone.

The weather in Toronto grew cold. The trees outside my window turned gold and brown, and in one night of wind lost all sign of life. The lake in the distance became a sliver of silver beneath a heavy sky. Now, no one came to the park. The view from my window was of desolation, of bared trees and deadened grass. I rarely looked out. My afternoon walks came to an end. Instead I went directly home from school, to my room.

I talked from time to time with Mrs. Harris and Mrs. Duncan. They spent almost every afternoon in the kitchen. They would drink coffee and eat cookies and talk about the boyfriends they had when they were young. How different from my mother, who could never acknowledge past boyfriends and could not even have a friend to talk to.

At four o'clock every afternoon Mrs. Harris would put on the little television and they would smoke and look at a soap opera. Sometimes they cried a little. I often felt, watching them blow their noses into tissues, that they were crying not for the people in the show but for themselves, for the people they might have been and the people they were. Their own lives were not so interesting as those they saw on television at four o'clock every afternoon.

I found it strange that they never told me their first names. It was as if they lost them. One cold, rainy afternoon, an afternoon on which shadows became airborne and floated about in the air, I asked Mrs. Harris why she called herself by her husband's name.

Stroking the cat, she thought for a minute. "It's tradition, dear. Christian tradition."

"Yes, dear," Mrs. Duncan said, "it's as simple as that. It's what women have always done."

"And what do you do with your own names? Are they no longer of importance?"

"A name is a name is a name," Mrs. Harris said. She lit a cigarette and the cat leapt from here lap with a growl.

I saw that Mrs. Harris did not like my questions.

Mrs. Duncan said, "Poor Ginger. She doesn't purr any more."

Mrs. Harris said, "She's gone off her food too." There was worry in her voice.

I went to my room. Through the window, the park hunched gloomily against the rain and cold. I thought of Ginger, and of my mother and Mrs. Harris and Mrs. Duncan, and I remembered the bird that would not sing.

That night my nightmare came again, but now I sense my own presence, and I no longer knew from whom--my mother or myself--came the sound of the weeping sea.

Two days later I received an envelope from my mother. I left it unopened for several hours: I feared what it might say and, more, what it might not. Finally, I ripped it open.

It was a short letter. In it, my mother told me that my father, on discovering my disappearance, had said nothing, had done nothing. He hadn't even called on his ancestors. She said that my father never mentions me. She then explained, briefly, the mystery of myself to me. She spoke of Michi, the idol of my father. Michi had been, my mother said, a strong and independent woman, a woman with her own ideas. She had been beaten into submission by my great-grandfather and was left, in the end, with little but her grandson, my father, as outlet for her sense of life. It was all my mother knew but she hoped the knowledge would help me.

The letter brought me once more directly before the life I had managed to ignore during these months in Toronto. It reminded me that I faced nothing here, that this life of freedom was one without foundation, that it would all inevitably end with a twenty-hour plane flight. That night I did not have my nightmare, for I did not sleep. I spent the night crying, and I could not understand why it was the memory of my father coughing before the Shinto shrine that caused me the greatest sadness.

Depression: the English word is inadequate to describe that which seized me, which took hold of my heart, my lungs, my intestines. This was more like a sickness, a sickness of the soul.

Two nights later it snowed. My coats were too thin for the climate. Instead of buying a new coat, I took out my return plane ticket.

When I arrived in Tokyo, it was raining.

I now work as a language teacher, instructing foreigners, mostly Americans, in Japanese. In return, one of them practises my English with me.

It has been over a year since I left my father's house. Since my return to Japan, I have telephoned my mother once, just to hear her voice. We both cried on the phone, but I did not tell her where I live. Not yet.

The sea no longer weeps in my dreams. Instead, some mornings I wake up with wet cheeks and a damp pillow. I do not know why.

Or maybe I do.

There is an English expression, "No man is an island." Or

woman. Expressions always contain a grain of truth and this is an expression I wish I had never learned, for it brings into too bright a light what I have come to understand: I am a woman, I am a Japanese woman-- I still look to the east when I take medicine--and the ties of tradition still bind me the way they bound Michi. To understand oneself is insufficient. Keisuke has yet to realize that his precept of refusing to let the past impede the future applies, in my country, but to one sex. This is, perhaps, why I failed to understand his poetry when I first read it: it was too alien in too many ways. Keisuke to one side, my father and brother to the other, but it is always the men. For them all, the common sentence: I am Japanese.

There is, as one of my businessmen students puts it, no leadership potential in me. I do not lead, I never have. I have only practised avoidance.

Accepting my father's values would make life easier for me. But I cannot do this automatically. I am not a clock. As a first step, therefore, I am taking a course in flower arranging, a small step, but important in its own way.

For I shall, I fear, return one day soon to my father's house, to the *Ko-to*, to the architects; for I have learned that the corollary of tradition's pride is tradition's guilt. Keisuke was right: I feel guilty for having betrayed my father's name and nine generations of ancestors. Keisuke helped me recognize my guilt but he did not equip me to deal with it. In this, and not in the seduction, lay the real betrayal.

Tradition designed my cage. My father built it. Keisuke locked it. In returning to my father's house, I betray my mother's faith but the load is lighter on my shoulders than that of the nine generations.

I shall pack away my picture book: it is a child's book. I shall save it for my children, my daughters and my sons. It is to them that I bequeath my dreams.

And in the meantime, I continue to arrange my flowers. Even a cage needs decoration.

11

Operation Cordelia

by
Réshard Gool

Born in London, England, 1931, Réshard Gool (deceased 1989) brings an extensive international experience to his writing. He was educated in South Africa, England and Edinburgh, and did his graduate work at McMaster University in Hamilton and the University of Toronto. Before joining the faculty of the University of Prince Edward Island, he taught political philosophy and fine arts at several other Canadian and West Indian universities. Founder and Editor of Square Deal Publications, he was active in the artistic and literary life of PEI and in Commonwealth Literature.

Where I start ought to be a matter of convenience and taste. But it isn't. I should begin with Grace--her birth (Weimar, 1923), upbringing and schools (England), war service (London, Canary Islands, Cairo, Ottawa, etc) and of course, her first love affair--but I hesitate. Aren't the Rassools, flourishing so glamorously yet vulnerably on the margins of defunct empires, equally important? Or the absurd transgressions of Crosbie which spawned international headlines? Or more important yet, the blandishments of the child, Sherine. A grown woman now, it was Sherine whose bait lured me into this narrative trap.

Sherine was originally pivotal, and later her patronage became dispensable. But in the end, it was Sir Robert Wilkinson who called my indolence and manifold ditherings to a halt; it was his death, and one or two events preceding and following it, which closed the trap.

The British press responded impeccably. There were no elaborate writ-ups. In due course a brief, untantalising *Times* obituary appeared. Wilkinson's schools and parentage were disclosed, but not much more. Sir Robert had read philosphy at the University of Edinburgh, patronised two London clubs, and cultivated an unspecified breed of roses. His Knighthood had come after World War II "for government service."

The BBC was equally discreet. So were the backrooms of Whitehall: except for fairly reliable talk that the prime minister had postponed a trip to Northern Ireland to get to the funeral.

The turnout was handsome. There were over a thousand mourners, and those unable to command a pew in the small parish church waited (under unsympathetic skies) outside, and left only when the last wreaths were laid against the graveside.

The wreaths looked expensive: the kind which countries lavish upon their war dead, and they hailed from all over the globe--the United States, France, West Germany, Scandinavia, Australia; indeed, no Commonwealth territory failed to send an appropriate tribute.

The Canadian wreath was impressive. But what stirred particular surprise was a combination from India--a small, white violet with a card no less enigmatic and incongruous. In one respect the card was not remarkable. Like most of the others, it bore initials only and the most general address of the sender. Eccentricity emerged first from what it asked, namely, that the small perennial be planted at, or at least near, the foot of the grave, and then within the following testimonial:

For "R.W."
with Love
1931-1947
A.R.
New Delhi, July'81

Not the most challenging inscription, I would have though; mildly intriguing, yes; nevertheless it excited Robin Boothroyd unusually.

"It's incredible!" he declared, "simply incredible!"

The disbelief used only a few notes above his range of discreet speech. There was no amazement in the way he sat, or in his eyes, which remained steadfastly thoughtful.

We had adjourned to a tavern called the White Hart, which (Boothroyd had confidentially impressed on me) was patronised by "the Glynbourne crowd." Except for a woman behind the pumps, the saloon bar was deserted so I assumed the place had just opened. It was a little after five-thirty, and still a bit muggy with promise of more rain.

"I expect," I said, "we'll have to get back by train."

Boothroyd waved the issue away. "My car's not far," he said. "I guess you'll have Guinness?" He took off his bowler and asked the woman behind the pumps whether she kept draught or bottled Guinness.

For himself he ordered dry sherry.

When the woman brought our drinks, I wouldn't let him pay.

"I guess you never met her," Boothroyd speculated, eyeing not me but his drink pensively.

"Who are we talking about?"

"Aisha Rassool?"

He looked up and seemed surprised that I wasn't tuned in to his mental wavelength. In the graveyard, I now remembered, he had stooped--not once, but twice--to inspect the eccentric card.

"I see," I said, "you think--"

He cut me short.

"What else?" he asked.

I didn't answer at once. Still too much ambiguity went an alternative I had in mind, so I used the occasion to expand my own information.

"You knew her quite well?"

"Matter of fact I did." Once again it was the sherry which held his attention. He turned the glass by its stem slightly, then back again.

"Cairo," I prompted, "wasn't it?"

"That's right," he admitted quietly, "Cairo, and once again, very briefly, in Addis. Or was that before Cairo? I can't remember." He looked up. "In Cairo she was quite a wheel, you know. Yes, indeed, quite a wheel."

"What was she like?"

"I liked her."

With Boothroyd one had to be patient. In his courteous manners, his soothing tone of voice, even in the only extravagance of an otherwise faultless wardrobe--a Pearson bow tie--he was plodding Ottawa.

"How old was she?"

Boothroyd frowned.

"Hard to say," he decided at last. "She was such a handsome, vivacious woman. Let's see. It was 'forty-seven when she died. I'd put her on the green side of fifty--not more than fifty-three, at the most."

"You were there when she died?"

"No. Her son was. What was his name? Very able young man. Zaid--that's it. It was in Alex at the time. That Alexandria. It's very hot in Cairo in the summer. Unbearable. He told me when I got back. He was in quite a state, quite distracted, poor fellow. They didn't get on well together, and I expect he felt guilty."

"Guilty?"

Boothroyd paused to weigh my question impartially.

"Yes. Now that she was dead, you see. It's a fairly common reaction--what could he have done?...If only?...You know the feelings?" I nodded.

"We had lunch at Shepheard's. He was staying at the Continental. So was I. But it was fashionable to eat at Shepheard's in those days. He had to take off that very afternoon, fly to Lourenco Marques--family affairs, I think."

"What did he do?" I asked.

Once again Boothroyd reviewed the question punctiliously.

"You know," he admitted at last, "that's an awfully good question. I guess you mean--for a living?"

I nodded.

He cleared his throat and took a sip of sherry.

"You know," he ventured at last, "I often wondered. They were independently wealthy, of course. The Rassools I mean. But Zaid was always a question mark. One day you'd bump into him in the muski--that's the native quarter--and he'd be broke as a dog, and he'd look it too. Then later you might catch him on Kasr El Nil wallowing in loot. Where he got it from, nobody knew. It wasn't his mother, that's for sure."

"Wilkinson." I suggested.

Certainly shook Boothroyd's head.

"No," he said, "he was a radical. That was his mother's biggest beef. They quarrelled about politics whenever they met."

"But wasn't she close to the Moslem Brotherhood?" I held two fingers together in the air. "Like that with them?'

Again his head shook with certainty.

"No," he insisted, "only with the Wafd. That's how she and Wilkinson fell out!"

"Oh, really," I said. "But she had worked for Wilkinson?

He didn't answer at once. He sipped again at his sherry; then he seemed to reach a conclusion.

"I can't say for sure," he said, "but I think so."

"Oh, c'mon both!" I protested, "you guys must have had tabs on her. You worked for the Brits."

"I worked," he corrected me, "with the Brits."

Because it looked as if he might become stuffy, I changed my tack.

"Why," I asked, "was Zaid going to Lorenco Marques?"

"Search me."

"I thought the Rassool headquarters were in South Africa."

Boothroyd disagreed.

"No," he said, "they had business everywhere. India, the Middle East, France--you name it."

"But he was going to Mozambique?"

"That's what he said."

"To sort out family affairs?"

"Ostensibly."

"And you believed him?"

Boothroyd shrugged indifferently; then he smiled and raised his glass. In between sips, he said:

"He was always very plausible."

as he put his glass down, he seemed to reconsider.

"It's strange," he said, "One never knew with Zaid."

"Knew what?"

"Knew--" he began; then burst unaccountably into laughter.

"What's the matter?"

The laugh became a smile; the smile became amusement which centred in his eyes and cheeks, and went--with his face--from side to side.

Because the smile seemed to involve me, I smiled, too "What's up?"

"You had me, didn't you?'

I was still unsure what he meant.

"You were just leading me on, weren't you? You may be retired, Jack, but you're still a reporter. What gets me is that you really had me going, didn't you?"

I laughed so as not to dispel his illusion too harshly, then I said:

"You're wrong, Booth!"

I chuckled now at both of us.

"It's wild!" I said, "quite wild."

His eyes interviewed mine skeptically.

"When I got a-hold of you, okay?"

"At the office?" he asked.

"No, no. Outside the cemetery. Just before we came here. Well, I knew exactly what I wanted to asked you."

"And you've forgotten?" he laughed.

"Rich, isn't it?"

"Was it the `A.R.'?"

I shook my head.

"No," I said, "I had that one figured out--hold on!"

I tended to rub my left eye when I'm tired or nervous or stumped. I did so now. I raised the rims of my specs so that they sat for a moment on the brink of my balding pate. Nothing. The questions remained just out of reach of the tip of my tongue. For a moment, his eyes watching mine over the top of his glass--his lips poised like someone about to sip or whistle--were distracting. Then I remembered.

Playing for time, I said:

"Like you, I got carried away!"

To know what to ask first entails knowing what to tell him, and how much. It was almost impossible to summarize my dealings with Sherine. At last I said:

"I'm toying with a book, but I can't decide whether to do it."

"What's it about?"

"That's just it," I said, with a wry chuckle, "the subject keeps changing every time I ask questions."

"Is it political?"

"In a way, yes. It started with the Gouzenko affair in 'forty-six."

"Did you cover the trail?" he asked.

"Not for CBC," I said, "I was freelancing then. But I did a number of magazine pieces on it. Nothing outstanding. The usual guff. Then I came over here and covered the Crosbie case--"

"The porthole murder! I remember that. When was that?"

"The murder, or the trail?"

"Both."

"The murder was October, 'forty-seven. The trail was about six months later."

"Not far from where we're sitting, " he said.

I nodded curtly.

"Sorry," he said, "keep interrupting."

"That's okay. It keeps me on track. At my age, I keep forgetting things.

He laughed as if he appreciated the condition fully.

"Let me try a few on you," I asked.

"Go ahead."

"Does the name Robinson mean anything? Bishop Robinson?"

He narrowed his eyes to think.

"Or Nigel? Nigel Robinson?"

"English or Canadian?" he asked.

"English."

"Nope. Can't help you."

"Okay," I said, "try this one for size: Colonel Hosein--"

"Farabi!" he exclaimed. "I knew Farabi. I knew him well."

"Did he belong to Wilkinson?"

"Good Lord, no!" he laughed sharply, almost cacophonously. "Quite the contrary. He was a militant, nationalist. One of Nasser's young, up-and-coming officers."

"A friend of the Rassools?"

"Of Zaid, definitely. Of Aisha? Maybe...I can't be sure."

"Okay. Last question. Did you ever come across a Grace Hawkins?"

"Grace *Hawkins*," he repeated, softly. "Grace--wasn't she Wilkinson's secretary?"

"I don't know whether secretary's the right word."

"Not his mistress surely?"

It was my turn to laugh.

"Hardly," I said. "I didn't think so myself," he said. "He wasn't the type. Oh, dear!"

I leaned forward, and in the same movement followed the direction that his dismay had taken. A group of swankily dressed, noisy Englishmen had collected--some on stools, a few standing--in front of the principal counter of the bar, and one of them--a tall, fair-haired man in a navy blue, pin-striped suit--was heading towards our table.

"What's up?" I whispered.

"Bad weather."

"How bad?"

"Just sit tight," he predicted grimly, "you'll see."

The Englishman was wearing a white carnation buttonhole and he swung his rolled umbrella in the air so that it landed, point up, slightly to one side of it.

"Weren't you chaps at the funeral?" he asked in a rude, nasal drawl.

"Yes, we were," Boothroyd replied considerately. Once again he was Ottawa, but this time I admired the candour and level-headed calm.

The man ignored Boothroyd.

"You're Easter, aren't you?"

"No," I said, with a chuckle. "No Easter this year. They found the body."

The joke took a moment to penetrate. When it did, the man's nostrils dilated to produce the sound of a horse simultaneously hiccoughing and neighing.

"Capital!" he pronounced. "Very good indeed! Name's Geoffrey Steele. Geoffrey with a *g*. Steele with an *e* at the end."

He stuck out a large, angular hand which I shook without enthusiasm.

"Hi, Geoff," I said, "that is--"

Steele interrupted.

"I think we've met," he said, accepting Boothroyd's extended palm.

"Canada House, aren't you?"

"Not quite," Boothroyd said, "But it'll do."

"Ah! said Steele, "security!"

He waited, but Boothroyd didn't answer.

"Have a pew," I suggested.

Steele considered me, then the chair I had moved by foot towards him.

"Thanks," he said, bending to dust the seat with one paw. "I think I will."

"What'll you have to drink?" Boothroyd asked, again the perfect Canadian diplomat.

"Let me get this," Steele insisted. He surveyed the table and called across the room in a loud, peremptory voice, "Same again here!"

Then, a few decibels higher: "And I'll have a shandy!"

When the woman smiled and nodded, he lowered his voice.

"Terrible service, these days," he muttered. "England's going to the dogs. Been like that since the war."

Just a trace of distrust flickered across Boothroyd's countenance, and I wondered whether he was also thinking that the man didn't look a day over thirty.

With a smirk, Steele said:

"So you're interested in Rassools, are you?"

Not just his impertinence bothered me. But it became strategic not to scare him off. I smiled and put on my guileless reporter mask.

"How did you know?"

"Gremlins, my dear fellow," he purred, "Lots of little gremlins scurrying all over London at my regal behest." He paused to smirk again, this time rather toothily.

Instinct told me that if I remained silent I might find out whether he was dangerous.

"What did you get at Somerset House?"

The question brought such relief that I felt almost condescending. On the other hand, it could be a trap.

"Not a whole lot," I admitted, and hesitated: an effective attack called for discreet phrasing. "Was Rassool a cover name?" I asked, again applying a mask of innocence. "Wasn't she in Wilkinson's net?"

My luck was in: he seemed flattered.

"That, she was," he answered, candid at last. "But up to a point."

"What d'you mean?" I asked, and realized that I'd been too truculent, too hasty.

His arrogance returned.

"I really thought," he declared, "you'd be able to tell me that."

I tried to remain unperturbed. I shrugged.

"Very well," he said. "Let me ask this then. What was Aisha Rassool doing in Ottawa a few years ago?"

Boothroyd started visibly.

"In 'forty-six?" he asked.

"No," Steele replied, angrily, "when you chaps sold India the Candu reactor."

"We gave India," Boothroyd said in a smooth tactful voice, "a Cyrus reactor in 1956. That was under Colombo Plan."

Boothroyd rose, looking at his wristwatch.

"I'm sorry," he said without any change in quiet benevolence, "you'll have to excuse us, Geoffrey. Nice meeting you."

He didn't shake hands, but I did, and thanked Steele for the drink.

It was mizzling outside; the tarmac and trees glistened under the street lights.

In the car, I congratulated Boothroyd on the timing of his departure but he seemed preoccupied.

He had started the engine and was letting it warm up.

"Who is this guy?" I asked.

"He writes for the tabloids."

"Features?"

"Yes. He writes his own columns. Potboiler stuff: 'Today at dinner with the prime minister...'--that sort of thing. He specializes in spies and scandals. The trouble is he's not stupid. Obnoxiously conceited. But he's usually well informed."

"Did you buy that one--" I began.

"About Mrs. Rassool?" Boothroyd interrupted. "That's just it. It's a puzzle."

"Like who sent the card?"

"I think he was fishing," Boothroyd said in the tone of someone thinking aloud. "I think the card bothered him. Just as it bothered me."

"And you don't have a file on Mrs. Rassool?"

Boothroyd didn't answer. He switched on his lights and wipers and eased the car out of the lot.

"Jack," he said, as soon as he found the road to London, "if I dig up anything on Mrs. Rassool I'll be in touch, that is, If--"

"If?"

"--if you let me see what you get. Deal?"

I laughed.

"Okay," I said, "You're on."

12

The Kumbh Fair

by
Iqbal Ahmad

Featured in ***Modern Stories From Many Lands*** *(1972), Iqbal Ahmad was born in Agra, India in 1921. After teaching at the Allahabad and Karachi Universities, he came to Canada in 1964. With a PhD in English Literature from York University, he was a Professor both at the University of Waterloo and at Ryerson until his retirement. His critical study on Northrop Frye is under preparation for publication. 'Kumbh Fair'(1969) was the first short story in English by a South Asian Canadian to appear in Canada. He lived in Toronto with his wife of forty years until his death in October 1993.*

For an hour or so Hamid had been trying to read. An open book lay on the table before him. He sat erect and read: "The same with the boys. First and foremost establish a rule over them, a proud, harsh, manly rule. Make them know...," then the words lost all their meaning, ceased to register on the mind. It was the late February air that was making him so drowsy. He had read that page he did not remember how many times and was still reading it at the end of an hour. He shook himself, got up and walked to the window.

The college buildings seemed to be sleeping in the Sunday quiet. The huge tamarind trees looked like shaggy monsters waiting to awaken some day. Under them a narrow gravelled road went zigzagging in the direction of the city. Dreamily Hamid contemplated the view, and suddenly discovered that he had been thinking of the girl in the prostitutes' quarter whom he had visited last month. Now he frankly gave himself up to thinking about her. He had had a lot of fun with her. She was young and good-looking--a healthy animal, probably a village girl. She was certainly new to the trade--the way she kept averting her face and resisting him. A feeling of voluptuousness came over him, a desire to press something. Moving from the window, he strolled to the mirror, and stood before it looking at his reflection. He had not shaved for two days and his chin was stubbly. He drew the back of his hand over the rough surface and smiled in response to some pleasant thought.

It was past eleven that night when he bribed the hallporter, the iron gate creaked on its hinges and he escaped furtively into the night. Outside it was cool and fresh and a breeze rustled the leaves of the trees which were ominously silhouetted in the dark. The sky was gemmed with stars. There was no one about. A bus passed him carrying only three passengers. Shortly he passed Madhu's corner. The blind beggar was still there keeping up with harsh monotony the repetition of the name of God. He seemed an untiring and articulate woodpecker, uttering the same cry hour after hour--Hari Ram, Hari Ram .... In the stillness the sound pursued him a long distance and irritated him. But soon he was out of its reach.

Here and there lights shone in some windows, otherwise the place was asleep. He passed the railway overbridge and entered the old part of the city. There was much more light here, and some shops were still open, mostly sweetmeat-and-milk shops and betel shops, where people sat on wooden benches drinking milk out of earthenware cups or stood chewing **pan** or smoking cigarettes and looking at themselves in the huge mirrors that decorated the betel shops. He went on. Street **ekkas** ambled past him. A rickshaw pulled up at his side, but he did not take it. He was in no hurry and preferred to walk. He reached the clock-tower which stood in the congested heart of the city. Stray cattle had herded under its shadow to pass the night. He looked at the motionless white heaps, and taking careful look around dived into a side-alley.

A fetid smell from the open drains greeted him, and a flower-seller hurried towards him to sell him a flower-chain. He was a young man, an emaciated dandy in a muslin **kurta** and green silk **tahband**, who had sacrificed his youth to the traders of love who lived here. Long, white jasmine chains hung from his arm. Hamid did not buy one, and the sharp smell of jasmine irritated him. There was little and broken light in the long alley, and some corners were completely dark. Here too business for the day had concluded, and those who had stayed on preferred the lights out. In a few low balconies some women still sat under the glare of electric lights, waiting. He looked up at them, at the overpainted faces and the inviting, entreating eyes. A sudden disgust filled him and he felt as if a shower of ashes had fallen over him. In his mind awoke the reek of sweet oils, cheap scents and stale perspiration. The underclothing had always been frowzy.

The occasional lights made sharp outlines in the dim alley. He passed on till he reached a door, where he knocked. An old woman opened the door.

"Is Vimla free?" he asked.

"Yes," said the woman.

"I'll come in," he said, stepping in. "It'll be for the whole night."

"All right. I'll go and tell her. We had finished for the night."

She opened another door and disappeared. He did not sit. There was a suffocating smell in the room. The old woman's sheetless bed was in a corner. The quilt was faded and horribly stained, and the pillow was shiny with layers of dirt and oil. She had spat freely and an area of six inches on the floor was messy with sputum in which showed yellow blobs of phlegm. He lit a cigarette to disinfect his nostrils and looked at the ceiling. It was so low he could have touched it with his hand if he were a little taller.

The woman returned. He counted out twenty rupees, and as he was going in she asked him for a cigarette. He gave her one.

The other room was much cleaner. Vimla was sitting on the side of her bed with her bare feet dangling. She had been lying in bed and had sat up to receive her customer.

"Oh, it's you!" she said, smiling.

"So you remember me?" he said.

"Why, of course, you were among my first customers."

"Was I?"

"Yes," she said and smiled again.

Then she grew serious as some reflection held her mind, and he watched her. She was looking far more beautiful and sure of herself than before. Last time, careless wisps of hair had strayed about her face and her eyes had a frightened look. She had seemed lost. Now her hair was tastefully braided, a trifle too oily he thought, and lamp-black darkened her eyes and tailed out at the corners. He did not like her.

"Shall we?" she said, breaking the silence and meaning to undress. She got up and had a drink of water from an earthenware pitcher that stood in the corner. A crumbled rose fell out of her hair. She pushed it under the bed with her foot.

Half an hour later she said in the dark, "What do you do?"

"I read, I'm a student," he said. He was blaming himself for paying for the whole night. There was no more desire left in him and he wished he could go away and sleep in the freedom of his own bed.

"Do you belong here?" she asked.

"No."

"You have come here to read?"

"Yes."

"How long have you been here?"

"Three years. One more and I'll be gone."

"I've been here two months," she said.

"I know," he said.

"How do you know?" she said.

"Wasn't I among your first customers?"

"Oh!" she said.

A breath of cold air swept in at the window and she, her head on his reluctant arm, shivered. "We came to the Kumbh Fair, my parents and I," she said hesitatingly.

"And you stayed on?" he said ironically.

"Yes, I stayed on," she said. "My parents were killed in the big crush."

"I'm sorry," he said, "I didn't mean to be a brute."

"I don't know whether they died or not, but I never saw them again. A hundred died that day," she said and added meditatively, "I hope they are dead."

He felt intrigued. Her last words were so toneless and calm that he did not know what to make of them. He heard her slow breathing.

"Why did so many people have to die? They had come to pray," she said.

"I'm sure I don't know. Maybe prayer doesn't make any difference," he said.

"Did you go there that day?"

"No, I didn't, but I read about it," he said. "The news papers carried everything."

The Kumbh was a bathing festival, and the third of January was the biggest bathing day. The Ganga, flowing from the foot of Vishnu and through Shiva's hair tumbles out of the Himalayas into the plains of Northern India, and touching scores of cities and towns and edging thousands of villages, joins the Jamuna at Prayag in its course to the sea. Here at the confluence of these two great rivers another joins them, Saraswati, an invisible stream cascading from heaven, and makes Prayag one of the most holy places in the land. The Kumbh falls every twelve years. Millions of people come to Prayag from every corner of India on this occasion, and have done so for over three thousand years, eager for a dip in the holy waters that would rid them of their sins and ensure their salvation.

Five million people converged on Prayag that year, making the assembly probably the greatest concourse of humanity in known history. Fifty special trains arrived every day; aeroplanes roared in the sky all times of the day and night and the high roads were alive with every type of vehicle ranging from the motor car to the bullock cart. Even then the vast majority of people had to come on foot. Along the railway tracks on both sides there were unbroken lines of people for a hundred miles. These men and women mostly tramped in silence, carrying heavy bundles strapped to their backs or slung on bamboo-sticks across their shoulders. Sometimes to beguile the weary hours they chanted holy songs. And all the time the overloaded trains thundered past them with people crowded on footboards and hanging onto the handrails, sitting astride on buffers, and precariously perched on the roofs of the carriages by the hundred.

At Prayag the river front for twelve miles had become a **caravansarai**. If you ascended a high embankment you saw a new town spread out like a map before you. The contracted river wound eastward through thousands of thatched huts that covered the white sands. At nightfall the design of the sprawling town flashed into view as electric lights went on and oil lamps were lit. Thousands of fires flickered in the dark and awakened mysterious feelings. Brahma may or may not be there, but there certainly was something in the air.

"A thin rain fell the whole night," she said. "We could not afford a shelter. The **sadhus** were overcharging so much, and we had but little money. My mother called them godless people, but my father told her not to complain; they had come to pray and not to grumble. So the rain beat on us and the wind was very cold. We shivered and prayed, and my father said that God was kind and he prayed that he might die there, for the fortunate who die there go straight to heaven.

"The bathing started much before dawn. In the morning the sky cleared and a bright sun came out. We had a dip in the river and were feeling very happy. I saw the hair that had been shaved off people's heads. I had never seen so much hair. A whole field was covered with it and it was removed by the boatful.

"As the morning wore on the crowd grew thicker and thicker, jostling and elbowing and pressing. We stood on one side and waited for the holy men to give their **darshan**. At last they came, riding on elephants and surrounded by naked **sadhus** brandishing tridents. The people in front formed a wall and the procession passed at a leisurely pace. The pressure from behind increased as more and more people poured down the embankment to have a closer view of the holy men. Then came a strong wave from behind that flattened the wall in front. Those who fell could not get up and were trampled to death. Such cries filled the air! People went mad, I think. They shouted and pushed and fell and walked on one another. Some got under the elephants' feet. I cried and could not find my parents. I saw a dead child and her eyes were lying out, and there was an old man, his belly had burst and people's heels went into it, and there were dead women, and some with child too. Oh, it was horrible! I was ready to faint, but I knew that falling was certain death, so I clung to those next to me.

"Is it true that a hundred died that day? More! Well, the situation eased off after a bit. In my helplessness, and blind with tears, I asked people if they had seen my parents, an old man and an old woman. Some did not answer, some said no. Then a man held me by the hand and said: 'Sister, there are some wounded lying on that side, come and look there.' He gripped my hand and I followed and we went through the crowd. I did not know what was happening around me and I walked as if in a dream. He took me into a hut, and suddenly turning round put his hand across my mouth. I was too dazed to realize what he was doing. He gagged me and tying my hands behind my back pushed me hard into a corner. I fell and struck my head on a stool. He muttered a few threats and said he would kill me if I stirred or tried to escape. I lay there in pain and fear, crying the whole day and far into the night. I knew I would never see my parents again. I was faint with hunger and crying, and weakness brought on sleep." She fetched a sigh and added, "He brought me here, and the rest of the story you know."

"Why don't you do something about it?" Hamid said with indignation.

"What can I do? Besides, what am I good for now?" she said.

"Oh, that's nonsense. Where's your home?" he asked.

"In Raipur. It's a village eighty miles from here. We walked." He thought in silence, and she continued, "I never dreamed I would ever lead such a life. But I suppose it was my fate."

"No, it's nobody's fate to lead such a life," he said angrily. "Look, why don't you get out of this, go home and live your own life instead of making money for this swine?"

She did not answer. He thought the man (who turned out to be the old woman's son) must have threatened to kill her if she tried to run away. How could he help her? Two thousand women between the ages of fifteen and twenty-five were reported missing during the fair. This was where they went. The police knew that inter-state gangs of kidnappers were active, and they were vigilant, yet...

"I dreamed of home only once in all this time," she said, talking again. "That night I had my first client. I knew he was coming and I cried my eyes out. They made me up. My head was splitting with ache. And then he came, a middle-aged man. He was stout and had grey hairs on his temples." She stopped as if to see him again in her mind, and said, "He was a kind man. He stayed for two hours. He must have been drunk. He held my chin and turned my face and viewed me from arm's length and said I was a **devi**. He seemed a nice man. When he left I was tired and fell asleep and I dreamed that I was home. My father was working in the fields and I took his mid-day meal to him. There was moist earth sticking to his hands. He was very happy to see me and pressed me to him and said, "Daughter, you have come! We looked for you everywhere, where did you go?" And I burst out crying, and clung to him and said, 'Why did you leave me like that?' I must have cried in my sleep, for when I woke up my pillow was wet, and the old woman sitting by my bed was crying too. She is not a bad person. She is always very kind to me."

"Of course, she'd be kind to you," Hamid said angrily. "You go on making money for them and they'll be kind to you. Kindness doesn't cost anything."

"No, it's not that," she said.

Hamid's mind was in a turmoil when he emerged from there and he thought furiously as he walked home. It hadn't grown light yet but he could sense the morning air. There was not a soul abroad. Even the human woodpecker Madhu was not at his station to break the stillness with the senseless repetition of the name of God. He reached his room and from time to time a vast emptiness revolved in his mind. He tried to sleep but could not.

At nine in the morning he returned to his previous night's rendezvous with a police inspector. They knocked at the door and were met by a thin, long-haired man. Knowing who they were and the purpose of their visit he asked them to come in. The old woman was in panic when she learnt why they had come. She rushed into Vimla's room saying that she would wake her up.

Vimla joined them in a few minutes. Her face was puffy and her eyes were heavy with sleep. Hamid smiled to her. But she did not return the smile. A flush came to her face as the questioning proceeded. He could not believe his ears when he heard her tell the police officer that she came of her own accord and the question of her going back did not arise at all.

"But you told me last night...," Hamid began, when she cut in sharply.

"Never mind what I told you last night." There was a hostile glitter in her eyes as she looked at him.

"But try to understand, I want to help you," he said.

"No one helps a prostitute. She has to help herself." She spoke bitterly in a tone that said much more than the words. It sounded like an accusation not of him--he seemed too small for that--but of something much bigger. He was quiet.

As there was nothing more to be said or done after that, they left. Outside the older man said, "You are a student, why should you get mixed up with such women?"

"I wanted to help her go home," he said.

"But she couldn't go home after what has happened," the older man said.

"Why not? It's not her fault."

"Who'll bother about that? She has been in the profession, and that's all that matters. By force or choice that's immaterial. Her reputation would follow her to the village. The accused man will see to it that it reaches there. What do you think her life would be like after that? The villagers would make it impossible for her to live there. Not only for her but for her parents too. No matter where she goes people would be cruel to her once they know her secret," the older man explained.

Hamid remembered her calling the old woman and some of the customers kind. Hers was a dirty, heartless world, but there was an occasional tear shed in it for her, and it was that which was holding her to it.

13

Fellow Travellers

by
Suwanda Sugunasiri

A Smith-Mundt Fulbright Scholar in the US to study linguistics at the University of Pennsylvania, Suwanda Sugunasiri was born in Tangalla, Sri Lanka in 1936 where his mother was a community leader and the father a respected educator and social activist. Immigrating to Canada in 1967, he earned a PhD in education from the University of Toronto. A co-founding editor of the ***Toronto South Asian Review****, he started his creative writing career in Sinhala, with two collections. A columnist in Sri Lanka, he writes to the Toronto Star and the Globe & Mail on Multiculturalism. His groundbreaking survey of the literature of South Asian Canadians (1980) in English, Punjabi and Gujerati (reported in* ***The Search for Meaning****, and the extensive Bibliography republished by the Multicultural Society of Ontario, introduced to Canadians for the first time the vast and rich literary resources of the community, and indeed some of the writers and critics that have since come to be known in Canadian literary circles. A classical dancer and stage actor, the Sinhalese play nari baanaa 'jackal son-in-law', directed by him, was selected as one of the ten best heritage language plays in Ontario in 1980. Most recently, he was featured in the NFB film, "To Canada with Love, & Some Misgivings." Suwanda is married to Swarna, and lives in Toronto with their two children.*

"Really,...what else?" said mother sarcastically.

Aunty Fair was returning from a visit to the hospital. "The nurse suggested that we buy Podihamy some Horlicks," she said, stepping into the house.

"How about some soup and hot milk and...and...my damn foot," chattered away mother as she turned over in bed.

Podihamy was ill for quite a while and had been taken to the Ayurvedic hospital. "She'll soon die of anemia," the weda mahattaya had said. "I froze when I heard that."

It was Aunty Fair who took Podihamy to the hospital every time she fell ill. This time, too, when diarrhea had set in. "Who is here to attend to her...? There is the Ayurvede... Why don't you take her there? She should be lucky to get away with diarrhea the way she pops into her mouth anything she can lay her hands on," complained mother. Podihamy rolled her bloodless eyes and looked at her like a mouse in a trap.

I cannot say when Podihamy first came to us. She had been with us from as far back as my memory goes. In answer to the hospital desk clerk's question, she said she was twenty-seven. Aunty Fair could not help laughing as she recalled it! Podihamy did not know her parents or anything about her relatives. She could not even say where she was born. Once or twice she talked of an aunt, but no one had ever visited her. Mother never failed to capitalize on this whenever Podihamy fell ill. "Oh, what a pity...where is you beloved aunt...? Has she taken another husband?" Podihamy would only look at mother for a while, and turn around meekly.

Podihamy had been at a certain Lillian's before she came to live with us. But not even Lillian knew where she came from. She had been picked off the street. Podihamy had left her, unable to bear the treatment meted out to her, the neighbours said. Her left hand had been deformed. Seeing Podihamy, a villager chatting with mother would say, "May merit accrue to you, fair lady, for taking this desolate one under your care," adding, "Podihamy, you should thank your stars that you are now in a palace." About a year later mother would tell such a woman, "She certainly no longer seems the helpless one she once was... You should see how uppity she is," adding, "What a pity I am bedridden."

For a long time Podihamy had been the subject of ridicule of the village boys. Wandering around with no place to go, she survived on food picked from trash bins. She would never hold out her hand to beg, and rarely did anyone buy her food. When someone did, she would eat silently, with not a glance at the donor. Her helpless eyes showed certain signs of anemia.

"It was the nurse, not Podihamy, who asked for the Horlicks," Aunty Fair explained.

"There's not a penny at home," said mother, straightening herself in bed. "Looks as if it's someone else who is more concerned," she murmured, casting a glance at Aunty Fair.

When I visited Podihamy the third day, the nurse repeated the request for Horlicks. Podihamy looked at me with pleading eyes as the nurse spoke to me.

"Maybe when there's some money around," replied mother when I told her of the nurse's repeated request.

"That'll be for ever," Aunty Fair intervened.

"Do you suppose we should pawn our valuables?

She knew it was futile to argue with mother. "What kindly people we are... for the past few days, we've not even bothered to see whether the poor woman is alive or dead," she said anyways.

"Well, there's the hospital, isn't there? If she dies, they'll take care of her," replied mother. Aunty Fair spoke no more.

"Let me see. I think I have some money saved for my medicine," Aunty Fair said after a moment, walking toward her room.

Aunty Fair was mother's sister. At the death of her husband, she came to spend most of her time with us. Although a successful businessman, uncle had not left much for her. They had no children. Her only possessions were a few antiques and her personal clothing. These she gave away to her relatives, saying, "Of what use are these now", but none cared for her. Her adopted son, now married too, turned a blind eye on her. Occasionally he sent her a few rupees but never once invited her over. Her sister-in-law's attitude toward her was irksome, so she found it increasingly unpleasant to spend too much time at her brother's. Finally, she stopped visiting them altogether and came to stay with us.

Working nonstop around the house, Aunty Fair became weaker and weaker in no time. She was already fifty. Still insisting on working, she started complaining of sickness. When she wrote to her adopted son, he undertook to send her five rupees monthly. An occasional sum of money from the brother supplemented her income.

Handing over the three rupee notes she had in her hand, Aunty Fair instructed the servant boy to buy a bottle of Horlicks.

"I don't think you need to go. Son has already been there.... The weather isn't that good either," said mother.

"So what if it rains...? Do you want me to wait until the poor thing returns home before buying her the Horlicks?" said Aunty Fair, as she went to the kitchen.

"Are we responsible for her diarrhea...? No wonder eating from dawn till dusk all the rice seeds and what not she can lay her hands on...! As if she has nothing to eat in this house... The filthy witch...doesn't brush her teeth...doesn't care to comb her hair...What an effort it takes to make her wash herself...Is it any wonder that she falls ill?"

"Her sickness hasn't got a thing to do with her personal hygiene...It is simply a case of anemia," retorted Aunty Fair, unable to contain herself.

"Well, now...why should someone get excited when I tongue-lash my servant," muttered mother.

Podihamy could hardly give up her habits after coming to stay with us. Although she now ate three hearty meals a day, whenever she went to fetch water from the street tap a few yards away, she would search the refuse bins for cigar butts, pieces of areca nut or some betel, and finding one, would immediately pop it in her mouth. A passerby, taking sympathy on her, would offer her a chewing betel. As if guarding a purseful of money, she would look around to make sure no one was watching before tucking it in her cloth. After a few stops she would place the pot on the ground and, again making sure no one was around, slyly reach for her chewing betel. Next, she would nibble at it for some time and, putting the whole thing in her mouth, start munching, like an ox enjoying a tasty meal in the cool shade. The fear in her eyes would disappear at such times. After an hour or so she would return home, her eyes darting about like those of a hunted animal. She would be severely scolded, or beaten, but the next time, too, she was sure to follow her usual routine. I have never seen her quicken her pace. Her deformed hand dangled on one side; with the other, she scratched her untidy hair. Aunty Fair would sometimes save her from punishment and take her to the well for a bath. Unable to make Podihamy mend her ways, mother finally came to abhor her.

Mother was often bedridden and unable to use the wash-room. Podihamy's specific duty was to attend to such needs.

Although kept away from cooking and laying the table, she was called upon to perform these duties occasionally, whenever the servant boy's services were not available. Sweeping the lawn and washing pots and pans were her duties; they did not call for speedy work. Sometimes, she would feign sickness, to spite mother I thought, but if caught she could not resort to such tactics for long. Mother would give her additional work. "As if we don't know what tricks she is up to," she would say, even when Podihamy's complaint was genuine. Podihamy responded by scolding mother silently; then, dragging her bare bones, she would move away, still muttering.

"There she goes again... there... why don't you pick someone else for your target?" mother would reply in return.

Podihamy's lip movement would become more rapid. It was faster when Aunty Fair was around.

Podihamy had been hospitalized a couple of times earlier for anemia. And, on medical advice, mother kept chewing-betel away from her. The physician had also recommended more nourishing food. "Not even we can afford to buy eggs and milk these days," mother would say. But whenever there was meat or eggs, Aunty Fair secretly saved a portion of her share for Podihamy.

"Golly, you should see her...clean bed linen...a bed with white curtains," Aunty Fair said, on returning from her latest visit to Podihamy.

"What's it to us even if she gets royal treatment?" said mother, in bed. "She must be quite a sight, I bet."

"Why do you have to pick on her all the time?" cried Aunty Fair, adding, "Why don't you send her away if she's that terrible?"

"What an idea... Who'll wash my bed-pans...? Can that little fellow do it?" And a few minutes later dropping her voice: "You know, it's sinful to get a fella to attend to such work."

"Yes, only that poor thing can do it," retorted Aunty Fair sharply. I have never heard her so cross with mother. With these words she retired to her room and stayed there till after dusk. Mother did not call her to dinner.

Upon discharging, Podihamy had been advised to rest for four weeks. Aunty Fair would now wake up with the crowing of the roosters to have bed-tea ready for us. "Where is the witch...? Must still be sleeping, tch," mother would raise her voice. "What's there for her to do...? Everything is ready," says Aunty

Fair. Working around the house all day long, Aunty Fair would go to her bed and massage her limbs for a long time, while the rest of us were sound asleep. When, finally, she went to sleep, she could be heard to moan.

With more housework and less rest, Aunty Fair fell ill a few days after Podihamy returned home. Her last pennies were spent on Podihamy, and now she had to do without medicine. Mother would not give her money either, suspecting that it, too, would be spent on Podihamy. And she expressed her anger by saying, "Ah...didn't I tell you...? Taking Podihamy on your shoulders...Who is there now to do all the chores?" Podihamy, weak as she was, attended on Aunty Fair as best she could. "You mustn't tire yourself," Aunty Fair said to her. Regardless, Podihamy attended on her with a devotion and interest she had never shown to mother.

Having ignored medical advice, Podihamy fell ill again. "Here we go again," muttered mother. Pretending not to hear, Aunty Fair moved Podihamy's bedding to her own room.

Aunty Fair lay on her bed, moaning. Podihamy lay beside her on the floor, also moaning. Aunty Fair was muttering something to her. As I passed the room, I stopped to listen.

"This is the fate that befalls helpless ones like us," she sighed. As if in approval, Podihamy turned her head toward Aunty Fair and fixed a look of gratitude.

Aunty Fair's condition was deterorating. The physician was summoned twice, and she recovered temporarily.

Podihamy showed a slight improvement, too. She was still anemic, however, and moaned persistently. Aunty Fair turned around to look at her. "What's it, dear?" Without a word, Podihamy looked into her eyes as if to say, "I am ill all over, but what good is it to talk about it?" Whenever she felt better, she attended on Aunty Fair over mother's objections.

With money received from her adopted son to buy medicine, Aunty Fair's condition improved in about three weeks. She could now sit up in bed.

As she recovered, however, Podihamy's condition worsened. There were early signs that this time would prove fatal. Mother summoned three physicians, but, Podihamy passed away in a week's time. During this last illness, Aunty Fair was a lost soul. She was too weak herself to attend on Podihamy, but whenever she felt better, she was with Podihamy. After attending on her, she would rest in bed twice as long. She still kept Podihamy by her bedside. Often, in the thick of night, she would light the kerosene lamp to observe Podihamy. "Is there anything you need?" she would ask, if Podihamy happened to be awake.

On the day Podihamy died, she had shown much improvement and talked a great deal. "I feel sorry for the lady," she said, casting her eyes downward. The lady was my mother. As she spoke, she wiped off a tear. "Fair lady, who will look after you if I die?" she said, casting her eyes low.

"What nonsense are you talking...? Why don't you go to sleep?"

"It is true that the lady beats me and scolds me, but it was she who gave me shelter," she spoke again, in a low voice.

She had incessantly spoken of Aunty Fair's illness, too.

"You mustn't tire yourself too much...You are too weak," she was heard to say repeatedly. "Tonight, I'll massage your body...I feel much better now."

She died a few hours later, her final look directed at Aunty Fair.

After Podihamy's death, Aunty Fair, was withdrawn. She had few words and preferred to eat in the privacy of her little room. But once as I passed by, she stopped me. "Sometimes I even see her," she said. "I hear her tender voice at times and look around." She would fix her gaze in a single direction for hours and hours, sighing occasionally. At bedtime, she recalled Podihamy. "Poor thing...That's what it's like, to be born with demerits past," she said in a low voice. "What an angel...Even on the last day her concern was us...May she be reborn to a better life."

Aunty Fair's health was now failing. Mother was disturbed. "How can you possibly get better," she said, "when you killed yourself attending on her? Sick ones should look after themselves." Aunty Fair listened in silence.

A few days later, mother was resting in bed. Aunty Fair entered the room. "I don't want to spend my last days here," she said, looking away. "The entire place is given to a lonesome darkness...Jayanta has been inviting me home for a long time...It is time that I go to him...After all, he is my adopted son....You have too much work yourself to be saddled with me." A tear dropped, and both looked away from each other. The next day, Aunty Fair was seen packing her few belongings.

(Translated from Sinhala by the author.)

BIBLIOGRAPHY

AHMAD, IQBAL
Fiction
"Time to go." *The Canadian Forum*, 1964.
"The Kumbh Fair." *Fiddlehead* 80, 1969.
"The Clown." *Toronto South Asian Review* 5.2, 1986.
The Opium Eater and Other Stories. Dunvegan, Ont.: Cormorant Press, 1992.

Bissoondath, Neil
Fiction
Digging up the Mountains. Toronto: MacMillan of Canada, 1985; New York: Viking, 1986.
"Insecurity." *Toronto South Asian Review* 5.1, 1986.
"Things Best Forgotten." *Literary Review* 29.4, 1986.
A Casual Brutality. Toronto: MacMillan, 1988.
On the Eve of Uncertain Tomorrows. Toronto: Lester & Orpen Dennys, 1990.

Dabydeen, Cyril
Fiction
" Across the River." *Toronto South Asian Review* 1.2,1982.
" At the Dawning." *RIKKA* 9.2, 1984.
" At the Going Down of the Sun." *Wascana Review* 2, 1981.
"At Your Peril." *Canadian Author and Bookman* 57.4, 1082.
"The Committee." *Toronto South Asian Review* 2.3, 1984.
"Everlasting Love." *Antigonish Review* 23, autumn 1975.
"A Far Place Home." *RIKKA* 7.2, 1980.
"Funny Ghosts." *Quarry* [Kingston, Ont.] 30, spring 1981.

The Glass Forehead Cornwall, Ont.: Vesta, 1983.
"A Kind of Feeling." *Antigonish Review* 44, winter 1980.
"A Mighty Vision from Punjab." *Canadian Fiction Magazine*, 1980.
"A Plan is a Plan." *Dalhousie Review* 62.4, 1982-83.
"The Puja Man." *Toronto South Asian Review* 5.1, 1986.
"The Rink." *Fiddlehead* 143, 1985.
"Something to Talk About." *Journal of South Asian Studies* 19.1, 1984.
Still Close to the Island. Ottawa: Commoner's Publishing, 1980.
To Monkey Jungle. London, Ont.: Third Eye, 1988.
The Wizard Swami. (novel) Yorkshire, Eng.: Peepal Press, 1985.
Dark Swirl. (novel) Yorkshire, Eng.: Peepal Press, 1988.

Poetry
Poems in Recession. Georgetown, Guyana: Sadeek Press, 1972.
Distances. Fredericton, NB: Fiddlehead Poetry Books, 1977.
Goatsong. Oakville, Ont.: Mosaic Press/Valley Editions, 1977.
Heart's Frame. Cornwall, Ont.: Vesta, 1979.
They Call This Planet Earth. Ottawa: Borealis Press, 1979.
Elephants Make Good Step Ladders: Poems. London, Ont.: Third Eye, 1982.
Islands Lovelier Than a Vision. Yorkshire, Eng.: Peepal Tree Press, 1986.

Anthologies
A shapely Fire. Oakville, Ont.: Mosaic, 1987.
Another Way to Dance. Oakville, Ont.: Mosaic, 1990.

De Santana, Hubert
Danby: Images of Sport. Toronto: Amberly House, 1978.

Gill, Lakshmi
Fiction
"An Excerpt from *Puja for Papa.*" *Toronto South Asian Review* 1.3, 1983.
"Excerpt from *Puja for Papa.*" *Toronto South Asian Review* 3.3, 1985.

Poetry
Exhausted Peacock. Vancouver: University of B.C, 1965.
Mind Wall. Federiction, NB: Fiddlehead Poetry Books, 1970.

During Rain I Plant Chrysanthemums. Toronto: Ryerson Press, 1972.
First Clearing (An Immigrant's Tour of Life): Poems. Manila: Estaniel Press, 1972.
Novena to St.Jude Thaddeus. Fredericton, NB: Fiddlehead Poetry Books, 1979.

Gool, Reshard
Fiction
The Price of Admission. Charlottetown, PEI: Square Deal Publications, 19733; revised and retitled as *Cape Town Coolie*, TSAR Publications, 1976.
Nemesis Casket. Charlottetown, PEI: Square Deal Publications, 1979.
"Operation Cordelia." *Toronto South Asian Review* 1.13, 1983.

Poetry
"In Medusa's Eye" and other Poems. Charlottetown, PEI: Square Deal Publications, 1972. Revised edition, Charlottetown, PEI: Square Deal Publications, 1979.

Itwaru, Arnold
Poetry
Shattered Songs. Toronto: Aya Press, 1982.
Entombed Survival. Toronto: William Wallace Publishers, 1987.
Shanti. Toronto: Coach House Press, 1990.
Body Rites. Toronto: TSAR Publications, 1991.

Kalsey, Surjeet
Fiction
"Confined by Threads." *Canadian Fiction Magazine* 19, 1976 Spring.
"Mirage in the Cave." Trans.author *Canadian Fiction Magazine* 36-37, 1980 Fall.

Poetry
Speaking to the Winds. London: Third Eye, 1982.
Footprints of Silence. London: Third Eye, 1988.

Mistry, Rohinton
Fiction
"Lend Me Your Light." *Toronto South Asian Review* 1.3, 1984.
Stories from Firozsha Baag. Penguin Books, 1987: Toronto: McClelland & Stewart, 1991.
Such a Long Journey. Toronto: McClelland & Stewart, 1992.

Parameswaran, Uma
Fiction
The Door I Shut Behind Me. Calcutta: Writer's Workshop, 1990.

Poetry
"Panchali's Hour of Choice." *The First Writers Workshop Literary Reader.* Ed. P. Lal Calcutta: Writers Workshop, 1972.
Cyclic Hope, Cyclic Pain. Calcutta: Writers Workshop, 1973.
"Trishanku." Toronto: *Toronto South Asian Review*; Madras: East West Press, 1988.

Drama
"Rootless but Green are the Boulevard Trees." *Toronto South Asian Review* 4.1, 1985; Toronto: TSAR Publications, 1987.

Persaud, Sasenerine
Fiction
Dear Death. Yorkshire: Peepal Tree Press, 1989.

Poetry
Demerera Telepathy. Yorkshire: Peepal Tree Press, 1988.
Between the Dash and the Comma. Toronto, 1989, unpublished.

Sugunasiri, Suwanda
Fiction
Yamayudde (Life Struggle) (in Sinhala), Gampaha: Sarasawi Publishers, 1961.
Meeharak (Idiots) (in Sinhala), Colombo: Gunasena & Co., 1962.
"The Ingrate." Trans. from Sinhala by author. *Journal of South Asian Literature* 2.4, 1966.
"Fellow Travellers." Trans. from Sinhala by author. *TSAR* 1.1, 1982.

Poetry
"The Snow and the Sun"; "Expectations." *TSAR* 2.2, 1983.
"Bridges." *TSAR* 3.2, 1984 Fall.
"Women on Tape." *TSAR* 4.3, 1986 Spring.
The Faces of Galle Face Green. Oakville, Ont.: Mosaic, forthcoming.

Vassanji, M.G.
Fiction
The Gunny Sack. (novel) London: Heineman, 1989.
No New Land. (novel) Toronto: McClelland & Stewart, 1991.
Uhuru Street. Toronto: McClelland & Stewart, 1992.